Foxhunt

The novel opens with a description of a day's hunting, a fox is soon found and the hunt that ensues turns out to be the run of the season. Derek Thyrde, a junior Whip in the House of Lords, would have had no great reason to dislike Sir Rupert Massingham, Bart., MP, MFH, the Master and amateur Huntsman of the Yardley Foxhounds who is also a rising star in the Tory Government, apart perhaps from the latter's interest in Derek's girlfriend, Julia.

But, a few days earlier, Derek had been asked to help Julia's stepmother, Dorothy, who told him that she was being blackmailed over a mistake made by her first husband many years ago. Lying in wait for the blackmailer, Derek had been appalled to see the idolised Rupert, of all people, picking up the ransom.

When Julia finally succumbs to the Massingham charm, Derek finds consolation in the beautiful Camberley Roberts who, it appears, has rather different reasons for being interested in Rupert's activities. As Rupert Massingham's career continues to soar until it seems virtually unstoppable, they follow the scent together. But can they convince Derek's political colleagues that their quarry is not the paragon he is universally believed to be?

In a dramatic climax, the Whip and the Master come together for – *The Kill*.

Foxhunt is a compelling and exciting tale of suspense, enriched by an evocative background of the hunting-field as well as some of the lesser known byways of Whitehall and Westminster. It is a splendid successor to *The Man Who Lost His Shadow* and *Two Thyrdes*.

by the same author
THE MAN WHO LOST HIS SHADOW
TWO THYRDES

Peter Tranter

from

Batu Dol

26. 10. 88.

FOXHUNT

Bertie Denham

**MACMILLAN
LONDON**

First published in the United Kingdom 1988 by
MACMILLAN LONDON LIMITED
4 Little Essex Street London WC2R 3LF
and Basingstoke

Associated companies in Auckland, Delhi, Dublin,
Gaborone, Hamburg, Harare, Hong Kong, Johannesburg,
Kuala Lumpur, Lagos, Manzini, Melbourne, Mexico City,
Nairobi, New York, Singapore and Tokyo

British Library Cataloguing in Publication Data

Denham, Bertie, *1927* -
  Foxhunt.
  I. Title
  823'.914[F]
  ISBN 0-333-48384-7

Typeset by Matrix, Covent Garden, London
Printed and bound in England
by Richard Clay Ltd., Chichester, Sussex

To
MICHAEL TYLER-WHITTLE
himself a former foxhunter, in gratitude for
all the help and encouragement in writing
that he has given to me over the years

The author would like to thank the following for their very kind help and specialist advice in relation to the writing of this book, whilst at the same time absolving them from the slightest responsibility for any inaccuracies that may have resulted from his own misapplication of the facts that they have supplied.

Michael Amberg, Esq.
The Lord Ampthill, CBE
The Lord Blake, FBA
The Lord Campbell of Alloway, QC
Sir John Colville, CB, CVO
A. S. Edwards, Esq.
Ian Gow, Esq., MP
The Earl of Halisbury, FRS
Professor Sir Alan Harris, CBE, BSc(Eng)
C. K. Haswell, Esq., F.Eng., FICE, F.I.Struct.E, FSME, Cons.E.
Brian Hind, Esq.
Divisional Officer Houghton, Northamptonshire Fire and Rescue Service
Mrs Ben Howkins, SRN
John McCririck, Esq.
Murdo McLean, Esq.
Geoffrey Parkhouse, Esq.
Captain R. E. Wallace, MFH
Chief Superintendent Sheila Ward
Miss E. Winder, Acute Unit General Manager, St Thomas' Hospital

CONTENTS

PROLOGUE

Saturday, 25 January

'HOLD HARD, DAMN YOU.'

The words, clear above the rising swell of hound music, came undiminished through the frosty atmosphere from where, fully three hundred yards off yet, the scarlet-coated figure was galloping down the wintry riding towards us.

Julia and I froze guiltily. We had been trying to slip unobtrusively down a rackway and out of the covert by a handgate, the dead leaves cracking under our horses' hoofs like thin glass eggshells. Even my seventeen-hand bay gelding, Asquith, stood rock-still.

Julia, beside me on her little chestnut mare, looked ravishing in neat black hunting-coat which, long and loose-fitting though it was, somehow emphasised every curve of her figure; perfectly tied stock; and bowler hat, the hair beneath it netted into a near-blonde sweep.

The cry of the hounds grew closer and louder as the figure thundered on towards us.

'Sorry, Master,' I said as he passed.

'Oh, it's you, Derek.' The suspicion of a grin flickered over his face for a moment. 'Well, damn you all the same.'

He took our intended route, cramming his horse down the overhung rime-tinselled rackway, and paused at the handgate to cheer his hounds out of the covert.

'Forrard away. *Forr-orr-orr-orr-orr-orr-orr-orr-orr-orrard.*'

He put his hunting-horn up to his lips and, with an almost identical rhythm, blew the equivalent call on that.

Then, glancing back briefly over his shoulder towards us, the horn still in his hand, he beckoned us forward with it.

'All right, you two, come on if you want to.' And he was through and away, leaving the small gate swinging.

Thankfully, we cantered off in his wake.

Long Mile Gorse, spelt like that but pronounced 'Goss' locally, took its name from the long straight hedge that led for fully a mile and a half from it to the place where the Yardley foxhounds had been kennelled at the beginning of the previous century. There was an enormous earth in one corner of it which had so many entrances that it was virtually unstoppable but, even so, Long Mile Gorse was reckoned to be the best covert in the whole of the Yardley country. It had been the first draw today.

Hounds had found almost immediately, and we had given the rest of the field the slip – including, I am ashamed to say, Sir John and Lady Elton, Julia's father and stepmother, who were staying with us and for whom we had arranged hirelings – because if the fox went away in the right direction it was vital to be away quickly. There was only one way out of the field that we were now in and that was a narrow hunt-jump at the bottom left-hand corner of it. It was known as Higgins's Rails – whether in honour of the benefactor who had first put the rails up, or of someone who had had a more than usually crashing fall at them since, wasn't quite certain – and although it didn't look very formidable, I knew from long experience that there was a drop at the far side of nearly a couple of feet.

I thought longingly of the flask at my saddle-front. I have long held the theory that no one is fit to ride a horse unless he has *over* eighty millilitres of alcohol in his blood, and a more than usually generous lawn meet seemed a long way back. But there was no time for recourse to it now; there were the rails looming and ominous ahead.

I needn't have worried.

Asquith adored timber; you only had to point him at a wooden gate or post-and-rails and you could almost hear the wheels whirring, the machinery beginning to turn. I crammed my top-hat down on my head, and he did this now, setting himself at perfect distance for take-off, and then we were airborne with that marvellous flying sensation. I leant back with one hand on the neck-strap to take the strain off the horse's mouth during the seemingly endless descent, and he and I were touching down, feather-light, leaving barely a hoofprint on the crisp turf.

I glanced back over my shoulder to see Julia landing safely, too.

'Good boy, Asquith,' I murmured, patting his straining neck with one string-gloved hand as we galloped on and away.

When I had bought him a couple of seasons before, he had been called Wait-and-See, which I had thought rather too pretentious a name for a hunter, so I had renamed him after the politician who had made that phrase famous. He was the best horse that I had ever owned.

The frost was on the surface only, and the going near-perfect, firm with just that little bit of give in it. Asquith was so brimming over with energy that my chief concern at the moment was to see that he saved at least some of it for when he would really need it later on. As we came over a low cut-and-laid hedge with a barely perceptible change in the rhythm, we could see the Master at the end of the field that we were now in, hounds having come to a check.

He glanced back and saw us.

'It's *him*, it's Old Lop-Ear,' he called out to us, the excitement in his voice unmistakable.

11

'Old Lop-Ear' was a fox who had gained a reputation for killing more lambs and poultry than any other in living memory, and this had been exacerbated by the fact that he was so easy to identify. While his right ear was erect in the normal way, whether through accident of birth or injury, his left flopped over, giving him a particularly villainous look that he fully lived up to. He had become infamous in this part of the Yardley country and, for season after season, farmers had been complaining of his depredations. More than one had sat up all night with a loaded gun for him, laid traps and even poison, but Old Lop-Ear had always been too clever for them. Long Mile Goss was a covert that he was known to frequent.

'Y't . . . y't. . . . '

The Master's full attention was back with his hounds again and he was encouraging them gently with a sort of soft intermittent chirruping sound, as they tried to hit off the scent. He was giving every impression of leaving them to work it out for themselves. But I knew that all the time he would be nudging them, systematically yet almost imperceptibly, towards the various directions in which his own experience, coupled with acute observation, told him that the true line might lie.

'Y't . . . y't. . . . '

The sun was shining now, and random noises of the countryside carried across the thin sharp stillness of the air with an amazing clarity: the strike of metal upon wood as two men drove in fencing-posts across the valley; a cur-dog barking in a far-off village; the distant crowing of a farmyard cock.

'Y't. . . . '

A single hound spoke. Then another. The rest ran towards them, nose to the ground, they too took it up, at first hesitantly but swelling progressively until it grew into a full-blooded chiming and they were off again, Julia and I after them.

Foxhunting means different things to different people. For some, it's merely an opportunity to ride across country, jumping everything in sight, and for these hounds and even the fox are almost an irrelevance. For others watching hounds work is everything and a horse is simply the most convenient vehicle to enable them to do so at as close quarters as possible. For me, it lies somewhere between these two extremes, incorporating something of each of them but how much more besides.

Another hedge, machine-cut this time, thicker and higher, and with a ditch on the take-off side, the sort you have to go all out for, and I sat down in my saddle propelling Asquith on into it and, again, he placed himself just right for it, rose and flew it, again that marvellous feeling and, again, we landed safely.

In any really great pleasure in this life there is an element of fear coupled with the satisfaction of overcoming it, and this is certainly present in foxhunting. Close after this come the spirit of competitiveness with fellow-participants; a sense of uncertainty – will it be a good day or a not so good? – an essential ingredient in any sport; and the best exercise in the world, leading to a feeling of total fitness and euphoria that enables one to leave all one's day-to-day worries behind, at least for the moment. But of one thing there is no doubt whatsoever: of anything approaching blood-lust or sadism, there is no trace at all.

Another post-and-rails, the take-off poached and deep. Again I put Asquith at it, and again he took off superbly but spattering poor Julia behind me with mud as he did so.

The relationship of foxhunters to the fox is a strange one. When not out hunting, there is nothing that they like better than to watch a fox going about his lawful, or more often unlawful, occasions. But foxes have to be controlled,

13

their numbers kept within limits compatible with the ecology and agricultural economy of the area concerned, and killing them cleanly with a pack of hounds in the open is not only the most satisfactory but also the quickest and, ultimately, kindest way of doing it. The death of the fox must therefore be one of the primary purposes of foxhunting, although at the end of a good hunt, for the field at least, it is often more gratifying to see a brave fox get away.

Across one of the few remaining ridge-and-furrow fields with its peculiar, almost seasick-making, sensation and out on to a wide green lane. An ancient farmer, bowler-hatted and gaitered, out for exercise on a grey cob, was ambling along towards me, his eyes turned in the direction that hounds must have taken. He looked down at the old horse between his knees for a moment and then shook his head sorrowfully.

I glanced at Julia, who had just pulled up beside me, and caught her eye.

'Poor old boy,' she murmured.

I took off my hat. 'Good morning, sir,' I said.

For answer he only pointed.

'Yonder he goes.'

I looked where he was pointing and was able to make out the diminutive figure of Old Lop-Ear, if it were indeed he, running uphill across the grassland some three fields ahead.

'Thank you,' I said.

We left him standing there, his gaze still fixed wistfully on where, the fox way out of sight now, a pack of equally diminutive hounds were streaming across the same field in his stead.

Over a line of three more sets of rails with long grass meadows between them, to the rhythm of our horses' movement and the sound of their hoofbeats over the turf beneath us, and then we ourselves were crossing the same field. Asquith's initial over-exuberance had worked itself out, and I now had that marvellous feeling that for the first time it was I, rather than he, who was in command.

Over the crest of the hill, and there in the distance I saw the familiarly shaped canvas top of a beat-up old land-rover, the property of Tom, Ted and Cully, the three Hunt Terrier-men to the Yardley Hounds, stationary in a by-road ahead. I had been watching out for them: they thought like foxes and rarely failed to anticipate the line that a hunted one would take, indeed, I had been rather surprised not to have seen them before this. The back of the vehicle, I knew, would be full of cage-like boxes holding four distinct generations of terriers, on each of whom was lavished enough care and love to do a whole family of children. But, as for the land-rover itself, the condition into which that had been allowed to deteriorate was pitiful, had it been a horse, it would rightly have inspired sackfuls of letters to the RSPCA.

There was a fairly solid-looking five-barred gate leading into the road ahead and I knew that they'd open it for me if I asked them. Somehow bravado took over. I put Asquith at it, again that winding-up, whirring sensation, and I was landing a matter of feet from them, standing in line as they always did, in the road on the other side.

'Well done, Derek,' said Tom on the right. They called me 'Derek' when I was alone with them, 'm'Lord' if anyone else was there.

'Well done, Asquith,' said Ted his brother on the left, ascribing credit where credit was really due.

Cully in the middle, no relation but their acknowledged leader, didn't say anything. He hardly ever did.

Too breathless to speak, I waved my whip to each of them and, as I jumped the ditch beyond into the first

15

ploughed field of the day, I heard the arrival of Julia into the roadway behind me.

'Well done, Miss,' said Tom and Ted.

Over a wooden fence and on to grass again, two more hedges, and then a fearsome-looking 'bullfinch', cut-and-laid originally, but thorns reaching out thickly from the top of it. I crammed my hat down and, shielding my eyes with one arm, put Asquith into it; he rose gallantly, there was a rending, rasping sound and we were through it and landing on to another ploughed field on the other side. Then, hearing an identical sound behind me, I glanced back to see Julia and her mare emerging together but, they not so lucky, parting company and both of them falling – in opposite directions.

The horse was up first. I reached out for her reins, just missed them and she broke into a trot and then a canter down the line of the hedgerow to the right. Luckily, there was a man working in it some fifty yards along.

'Loose horse,' I shouted.

He waved a hand in acknowledgement, caught the mare expertly and started leading her back towards us.

Julia was on her feet again now.

'I'm all right. Don't wait for me.'

I stood on, irresolutely.

'Go on, you fool, or we'll both lose them. Don't you see, it's our only chance. If you can keep in touch with them, I will with you, and that way I'll be able to catch up with them yet,' she said.

She was right, I could see that. I didn't need any more urging, I cantered off over the ploughing. Three more fields, luckily grass, and the Master, hounds well ahead of him, was in sight again.

Asquith was still going strongly. A formidable-looking hedge with a ditch towards and he took off and flew it. I looked down as we were passing over and saw to my horror a mat of barbed wire interlacing the top of it, but it was too late to worry, we were landing and on again.

There were three of us again now: we had been joined by a girl in a dark blue coat and hunting-cap, very pretty with a noticeably pink and white complexion, wearing a distinctive hunt collar of light blue and white diagonal stripes. I remembered seeing her getting out of the Master's Range-Rover at the meet – she must have been doing point duty at the corner of Long Mile Gorse to have avoided being left like the rest of the field.

We jumped the next hedge, a high wide thorn hedge, together. She and I rose and flew it in unison, a smile of pure joy on her face; and as we landed, neck and neck, and drummed on forward she caught my eye and rolled hers upwards.

'What was that worth?'

'I couldn't put a price on it,' I said.

I had reached that most satisfying stage where I had become moulded into my horse so that we were almost part of one another. Asquith was jumping like a dream. Over a high hedge, with a machine-dug ditch on the landing side – we had eighteen inches to spare at that one – on to a concreted farm road and there was a metal gate, strong and unyielding in front of me, no time to open it though, over and through the muddy farmyard, out and over a similar gate on the other side. On to grass again, across and over a stile on to a road and, turning right, along the main street of a village still at a gallop to the ringing of iron on tarmac, inhabitants coming to door and window and waving as we went by.

Left through an open gateway, across that field to another five-barred gate, slightly less high and much less solid this time. But, when I put Asquith at it, either he wasn't looking properly or somehow he just hadn't got the energy.

There was an almighty crash and the whole thing dissolved into fragments.

I glanced back apologetically at the girl in the distinctive hunt collar, but she only smiled and waved a thankful hand to me. The standing tariff for breaking a gate in the Yardley country was fifty pounds to cover the cost of replacement. Luckily there were no stock in either field to worry about, so I just made a mental note to drop in a cheque on the farmer on my way home.

One more field, and hounds had checked again. The Master was sitting motionless on his horse. His gentle 'Y't . . . y't . . . y't . . . ' was the only indication that he was again engaged in casting them.

Thankfully, I drew to a halt behind him, took out my flask and passed it to the girl in the distinctive hunt collar. Then, when she had handed it back to me, I took a long swig myself. Extraordinary, I thought, how when one is hot and tired out hunting, neat whisky is the best-possible thing for quenching one's thirst. Asquith, ears pricked up, was watching hounds work as he always did. I took his packet of Polo mints out of my breeches pocket, leant forward in my saddle and fed him three.

'Y't. . . . '

Suddenly I noticed, away to the left, that invariable giveaway to a hunted fox, a herd of bullocks bunched on a hillside, heads erect and gaze fixed to the front of them. I looked in the same direction and saw the figure of a man on the far skyline, clearly outlined against the light behind him, with his hat held high.

'Holloa over there, Master,' I shouted.

He turned and looked where I was pointing.

Then he gathered his hounds together and cantered off with them in that direction. 'Huic holloa, huic holloa, huic holloa.' The leading two soon acknowledged the line, and others took it up. But a hare chose that of all moments to get up right in the middle of them and run off zig-zagging, three and a half couple of young hounds setting off blithely in pursuit.

' 'Ware hare.' The Master had reined in slightly. ' *'Ware ha-a-a-a-re,*' he rated again, but to no avail. He turned in his saddle and looked back in our direction. 'Go and get those back, will you?' And he galloped after the rest, who were off on the true line to the most beautiful, the most evocative music in the whole world, a pack of hounds in full cry.

'Oh, hell!' I thought and prepared myself resignedly to obey his instructions. But then I caught the eye of the girl in the distinctive hunt collar. She gave an exaggeratedly servile salute with her whip in the direction of the Master's receding back, murmured, 'Yes, sir, very good, sir,' cast a half-amused, half-exasperated look in my direction and cantered off after the errant hounds, leaving me free, thankfully but somehow a little guiltily, to carry on after the main pack.

I was completely lost now – I never did have much sense of direction. Asquith, foaming at neck and flanks, was labouring gallantly and, as for myself, I was lapped in that glorious feeling of tiredness unique to foxhunting, which is made up of total physical exhaustion combined with total mental alertness. My red coat was bespattered, its brass hunt-buttons – the Yardley 'Y' surmounted by a marquess's coronet inherited from an earlier Master – caked with mud and my string gloves, once white, had taken on a uniform beige colour, soaking wet and having that strangely attractive ammonia smell that comes from a horse's sweat.

Nursing a tired horse home in the closing stages of a hunt is something akin to riding an old-fashioned single-geared bicycle up a long steep hill and it was with very much this sensation that, standing on my stirrups now, I steered Asquith in the tracks of the Master's horse just in front of me, almost lifting him over jump after jump by the reins.

It was thus that we came to the most formidable set of post-and-rails yet.

And then, suddenly, I did know where I was. It was Higgins's Rails, that first drop fence, again, but this time from the other side. We had come round in an enormous circle back to Long Mile Gorse.

Horse and rider in front of me charged at the obstacle and were over it, but with an explosive cracking sound as the top rail disintegrated, lowering the fence by a foot or more for Asquith and me. Even so, we rapped the next-highest hard enough but we too were over safely and just in time to see Old Lop-Ear being pulled down in the open and disappearing from sight into a seething mass of black and white and tan, not five yards from that part of the covertside where one of the entrances to the great earth lay.

As we came to a halt alongside them, the Master slid from his saddle, threw his horse's reins to me and, plunging both arms into the mêlée, withdrew the dead body of the fox.

There was a woman on a horse coming through a gate in the hedge to the left of us, and at first I thought that it was the girl in the distinctive hunt collar. But she had no hounds with her, and I soon saw that it was Julia, caught up with us again just as she had predicted. She couldn't have been far behind us all the way.

I got down off Asquith myself and, as I stood there, the steam rising from the horses' sodden flanks into the cold of the atmosphere formed itself into a mist-cloud around us. The Master produced a clasp-knife from somewhere and cut off the two main trophies, putting the mask with its famous lop-ear into his own inside coat pocket and tossing the brush to me.

The occupants of every sheep-fold and chicken-roost for miles around, to say nothing of their proprietors, would have cheered – could they have been there to see it – as he threw Old Lop-Ear's body to the hounds.

'*Who-whoop*,' called Sir Rupert Massingham, Bart., MP, MFH, and he took out his horn again and blew the long single quavering note, sad but triumphant, of 'The Kill'.

He was a man who had achieved distinction early in a number of diverse fields. As a Master of Foxhounds, he was reckoned among the three or four best amateur huntsmen of his generation. As a politician, he was set on a course that many people believed would lead him to Number Ten – and in the not too distant future, at that. As a man, he was liked, revered even, by other men; while, as for women, all the single girls in the Yardley country were after him, as well as half the married ones. Julia herself was besotted over him already.

He was also, I knew, although he didn't know that I knew and I was far from being able to prove it, a crook – of the meanest and nastiest kind.

I

THE FIND

Tuesday, 21 January

There are twelve tunnels under the River Thames in Greater London.

Two of them have been closed to the public since the beginning of the century: the Tower Subway and that which once served the old City and South London Railway. Five more form part of the London Underground Railway system, one on the Metropolitan Line, Brunel's original Thames Tunnel, two on the Northern, Charing Cross and Bank routes respectively, and one each on the Bakerloo and Victoria Lines. British Rail contributes the one used by 'The Drain' on its way from Waterloo to the City. Then there are two road-tunnels, Rotherhithe and Blackwall, for pedestrian as well as for motor traffic. The Dartford Tunnel is out of the area, of course, so it is the two footways, Poplar to Greenwich and Woolwich to the Isle of Dogs, that make up the twelve.

Twelve that are generally known about, that is.

It was only by sheer chance that I myself discovered the existence of the thirteenth.

Some weeks before, I had bought a house in the Clapham area of South London, in which I had installed Julia Elton, my girlfriend on and off over the past seven years – at the moment it was marginally more on than off – and the contents of the flat that we had been sharing.

I was driving from this along the Wandsworth Road in the direction of Westminster when I saw the car again. It was a common enough silver-coloured BMW, and its registration number, DWK 49 T, would have been totally unmemorable to almost anyone except for myself. But 49 had been the number allotted to me at my private school – 'T' standing for Thyrde, of course – and, as for the opening letters, at one stage during my progress through that establishment I had been nicknamed 'Dewek', on the grounds that I couldn't pronounce my 'R's properly – a calumny which even now I indignantly deny.

Twice before I had noticed the BMW in front of me among the traffic build-up due to roadworks that seem to be a perennial feature of this road, and each time it had turned off towards the river down a particular street to the left. On the second occasion, when I had eventually crossed Vauxhall Bridge and turned right along Millbank, I was pretty sure that I had seen the same car again, now even further ahead. I couldn't be sure, of course, because it had then been some fifteen or twenty cars away to the front but, if it were, the driver obviously had some short cut unknown to me.

This time, I decided to follow it, if it should take the same left turn again. It did.

It took me down a long hill, right at the bottom, then left, then right again. We were now in the street that runs nearest to, and parallel with, the River Thames, but almost immediately it turned off the road through some wooden gates on the left which shut behind it. I was in no particular hurry, so I stopped my own car and got out. Somewhat ashamed of my curiosity, I walked over to the gates, which had a faded notice painted on them: 'WARNING. GUARD DOGS IN OPERATION.' I peered through a gap and was just in time to see the BMW disappearing through an opening in the wall facing me of a tall warehouse building, which must have stood fairly close to the river ahead.

So much for my guide, I thought. But when I got into my own car and drove on, the road ahead of me was virtually clear of traffic and, when I rejoined Wandsworth Road at Nine Elms, having bypassed the roadworks, I reckoned that the diversion might well have saved me time if it hadn't been for the stop. I was on my way to visit Lady Elton, Julia's stepmother, at her flat in Marsham Court.

Her husband, Sir John Elton, had rung me up from his office in the City early that morning. It had been through him that Julia and I had first met when he was Shadow Home Secretary. I myself had been a junior Opposition Whip in the House of Lords then.

'I'm worried about Dorothy,' he had said. 'She hasn't been herself for days and I know she's worried about something. But every time I ask her she not only won't tell me, she swears there's nothing wrong at all. Just drop in on her this morning, there's a good fellow. For God's sake don't let on I've talked to you, but there's just a chance you may be able to fathom out what it is.'

It was with this rather nebulous commission very much on my mind that I drove over Vauxhall Bridge and pulled up, having just failed to make the lights for the right turn at the far end. I sat there waiting, idly watching the cars that sailed across in front of me from the left. The very first one was unmistakably the silver-coloured BMW, registration number DWK 49 T.

I cast back in my memory in an effort to recapture the scene that must have been imprinted on it by the briefest of exposures obtained just a few minutes before through that gap in the wooden gates. A rectangular yard, twice the length of a cricket-pitch, sloping down to the tall building at the far end, with its opening just off-centre to the left.

24

There had been no sign of any guard dogs, the faded warning notice must have been long redundant, but the yard had not been quite empty; there had been a dark blue van parked over to the right. I remembered now a fleeting impression, rejected as over-fanciful even as it arose, of the opening in the grey wall resembling the mouth of a tunnel. But hadn't the headlights been turned on as the car went into it and, was it my imagination, or hadn't it seemed to be continuing on a downward slope as it disappeared from sight?

One thing did seem certain: it really wasn't possible for the BMW to have come out of the gates again, gone all the way to Chelsea Bridge, across it and back along Grosvenor Road, and reached this junction by the time that it did.

There had been a name painted on the side of the parked van which I remembered striking me as being a particularly odd one at the time, but which I was totally unable to recall now. And, hard though I tried, as the lights came round full cycle and I was able to let in the clutch and continue on my journey I had an equal lack of success all the way to the Eltons' flat.

Dorothy Elton opened the door.

Worried or not, there was nothing strained or artificial about the smile of welcome that immediately erupted.

'Good morning, *Lord Thyrde*,' she said. 'Derek, how lovely! Do come in.'

Not very much older than me, the hair which had been an entrancing red roan colour when I had first met her shortly before her marriage to John had faded in the few years since to what I can only describe as a flea-bitten grey. But the words are totally inadequate to convey the impression of the curls that framed her endearingly urchin face. I kissed her in what I hoped was a sufficiently platonic manner and followed her in.

25

If she hadn't been Julia's stepmother, now ... to say nothing of being John's wife.

The drawing-room exuded the sort of comfort that goes with chintz and walnut and old gilt. I knew that Dorothy had had a totally free rein over its decoration and furnishing as soon as they were married, but its atmosphere reflected not so much her own personality as her interpretation of John's. We sat in armchairs on either side of the fireplace, a long low table in between.

'John's out, I'm afraid,' she said. 'Had to leave early for the office; he's going to Bobby Digby's memorial service at twelve. Oh dear, the poor old Tories aren't having a very good time of it at the moment, are they?'

I shook my head. For some months the Government had been going through a more than usually accident-prone phase, and Bobby Digby had only been the latest manifestation of it. A promising young middle-ranking minister, he had been caught out in a sensational affair with an actress. She was known universally by her stage name of Honoria, she must have had a surname I suppose, but if she had nobody was ever aware of it, and she was very beautiful and totally promiscuous. I had had to confess to myself at the time that I couldn't quite answer for what I would have done in similar circumstances but, as a relatively junior government whip in the House of Lords, I hoped I still hadn't quite reached the zone for political scandal. But it hadn't only been the sex angle, even though the Opposition had held up self-righteous hands in horror at that, there had been security implications as well. Honoria was an ultra-left-wing activist – financed, it was alleged, from goodness knows what source – and that had brought in the more vociferous Tories, too. There had been no alternative but for Bobby to resign immediately, and it had seemed likely that it was also going to cost him his marriage when, driving back to his constituency late at night along the M40, he had run into the back of a slow-moving lorry. He had been killed instantly, but nobody else had been hurt.

Bobby Digby had been the man who had taken over Gloucestershire East, John Elton's constituency, at the by-election when, as Shadow Home Secretary, he, too, had had to resign both appointment and seat towards the end of the last Labour administration. Since then he had become a close friend of the Eltons. Dorothy had been devoted to him – indeed, it had been her last-minute and highly uncharacteristic announcement that morning that she wasn't going to go with him to the memorial service that had finally triggered off John's telephone call to me.

'Do you think it *was* suicide?' I said. There had been some talk about it as well as a lot of very guilt-ridden faces among all parties in the House of Commons since.

'I don't know. Either that or just that he wasn't paying attention to his driving due to worry over that wife of his forever getting at him. Does it matter? I've no patience with Jenny, probably drove him into the affair in the first place and, even if she hadn't divorced him, she'd have got the maximum mileage out of it and made his life unbearable, horrid little prig. I'm not saying I'd be overjoyed if John had a go with that Honoria woman – not that he's likely to, bless his heart.'

Dorothy paused in thought for a moment or two.

Then: 'He'll see all his old friends there this morning, that's one thing. He feels so out of it all, poor lamb. I try to make it up to him, but he misses politics, you know.'

She stood up. 'Coffee?'

'I'd love some.'

'By the way, how's Julia?'

'Fine, thanks.'

27

At the door she turned. 'I do wish you two would hurry up and get married. You *know* how your present arrangement worries John,' she said.

This was getting far too personal for comfort. For myself I'd have welcomed it, but things had somehow been going far from well between myself and Julia lately and I wasn't too sure how she would react to such a suggestion just at the moment. All the time that clinking noises were going on in the kitchen next door, I searched frantically for some means of changing the subject. Suddenly the name that had been painted on the side of the van in the warehouse yard flashed into my mind. I could visualise it quite clearly now – the paintwork had looked brand new in complete contrast to the guard-dog notice on the wooden gates.

Dorothy Elton reappeared through the doorway carrying a tray. 'It's only Nes, I'm afraid. As I was saying, don't you think—?'

'Have you ever heard of a firm called Glocksfoot Restorations?' I said.

As a diversion it succeeded dramatically.

She paused in her step for the briefest of moments, her smile vanishing instantly. Then, very very slowly, she walked expressionless over to the table, lowered the tray on to it with meticulous precision and sat down. There was a plate of home-made shortbread, thick, crumbly and delicious-looking. She poured out two cups as though she were attempting the most difficult thing in the world but was determined to do it well and, still without a word, handed one to me.

Then she held out the plate.

'Biscuit?'

'Not for me, thanks,' I said with a pang of real regret. I still had three-quarters of a stone to lose before the Hunt point-to-point in March.

Dorothy stirred the coffee in her own cup round and round and round, even though there was no sugar in it. She put the spoon down in the saucer but she didn't pick up the cup. She just looked at it. Then she looked up at me with all the gravity of a bewildered child.

'What . . . ? That name you said just now. What do you know about it?' she said.

I told her. Seeing the BMW again, how I had followed it, the van, the name painted on it, the thing that looked like a tunnel and how the car had mysteriously reappeared on the other side of the bridge.

When I had finished: 'And that's all?'

'That's all,' I said.

There was another long silence.

'Tell me about it,' I said gently.

'Look, Derek, if I do tell you' – she was speaking very quickly now – 'do you promise, swear, not to tell anyone, anyone at all – not Julia, not John, especially not John, least of all the police?'

This put me in something of a quandary. I had come here specifically at John's request, to find out for him what was the matter. So how *could* I promise? But, if I didn't, I was pretty sure that she would clam up completely, and what good would that do? I might at least be able to be of some help, to her *and* to John, if I did know – even if I couldn't tell him.

'I suppose so,' I said.

'Swear?'

'I swear.'

Then she began to tell me.

'I know it sounds ridiculous. Me of *all* people. But . . . I'm being blackmailed,' she said.

It had all started some twelve years before. She had been married to her first husband, George Hanworth, then and

29

they had been running a pig farm in Gloucestershire which was in deep financial trouble. George, a solid bull-terrier of a man, had known for a certainty that if only he could put enough new money into it he would soon turn the corner, but the bank had been adamant. Dorothy had been able to see their point even at the time – the Hanworths had already been mortgaged and overdrawn to the limit – but then they didn't know George. She did.

'You never met him, did you?'

'No,' I said.

'You'd have liked him.' She was staring at the picture over the fireplace with an intensity that a Herring farmyard scene didn't quite merit just at that moment – even though it did feature a pig.

Then she went on.

In desperation they had thought of one of their neighbours, Wally Bagley, a blunt self-made man from Birmingham, who had come to retire nearby and who looked on the Hanworths as his entrée to local society but seemed to be genuinely fond of them as well. Certainly they liked him. They went to see him. He agreed to lend them the money, and at a reasonable rate of interest, too, but Wally hadn't got where he was by taking unnecessary risks. The one thing that Dorothy, either of them, for that matter, had of any value at all had been her set of family diamonds – necklace, ear-rings, bracelets, the lot – and the old boy had seen her wearing them on one occasion and he suggested now that these should be used as security. George had refused even to consider the idea, turned it down completely at first; it had been Dorothy who had insisted. A local solicitor had been brought in to draw up the deed and this, together with a photograph of the jewellery and a valuation by a reputable firm, was kept by their benefactor – Dorothy continuing to keep, and on occasion wear, the diamonds. It was a very happy, if informal arrangement.

There had only been one snag. The jewellery was entailed – of course the solicitor ought to have satisfied himself as to the true state of ownership, but apparently he hadn't done so – and, as she and George had no children, it was destined to pass eventually to a distant cousin. It was only hers for life.

As for the Hanworths, they had both been so confident that they had hardly even considered that aspect of it. Things were bound to get better. They both knew that.

'And things got worse instead?'

'No,' said Dorothy, 'looking back on it now, that's the amazing thing. They really did get better.'

Indeed, from that moment the farm had picked up so well that they would have been able to pay off everything in a matter of years, had not George suddenly and quite unexpectedly died of a massive coronary. The heartbroken Dorothy had sold the farm, repaid the loan from their kind old friend and subsequently met and married John. And that had looked like being the end of the matter.

Soon after her second marriage, the Eltons had gone to dine with Wally Bagley. John had wanted to thank him personally for what he had done for his new wife. In an expansive moment after dinner the old boy, who was clearly delighted that he had been able to be of such help to someone who was now the wife of Sir John Elton, had taken the papers out of an unlocked drawer to show to them. It did occur to Dorothy at the time that perhaps she ought to ask for them back, but somehow she hadn't had the heart to. He took such an obvious pride in them and, in any case, why worry? As far as the payments of interest and the return of the loan itself were concerned, she still had all the proper receipts.

That had been nearly six years back. Three weeks ago, Dorothy had received the first telephone call – the second had been early this same morning. The caller was now in possession of the papers. What her husband had done had not only been dishonest but criminal as well and would have warranted a prison sentence. Surely it would be a pity for his name to be blackened after all this time. She had exactly three weeks to pay, or the papers would be sent to the Press.

Dorothy looked up at me helplessly.

'He was right, too. I didn't believe him at first, but I rang up a lawyer friend – putting it as a hypothetical case, of course – and he confirmed it. George really could have gone to prison. I still don't see why, though. The diamonds are mine for life; we only wanted to use them as security for a year or two and we knew we could pay it all back. What's so wrong about that?'

'Well,' I said, 'if things had continued to go badly, you could have lost all his money, too, and it would have been unsecured.'

'Yes, but they didn't,' said Dorothy with total feminine logic. There really didn't seem to be much point in even trying to argue with that one.

The second call, early this morning, had been merely to give instructions as to how the money was to be handed over. It was to be left later in the day in the back of a parked van with that Glocksfoot name painted on it, but Dorothy flatly refused to tell me where or when.

'It's not that I don't trust you, Derek, but I really daren't tell even you that.'

'Could this old friend of yours be the blackmailer himself?'

'Wally Bagley? Not in a hundred years. He didn't ever marry, and I'm quite convinced that he came to look on George and me as the children he never had.'

'Er . . . I hate to ask you this,' I said, 'but just how much is it you're being blackmailed for?'

'Fifty thousand. That's exactly the same amount as the original loan, worth a good deal less now, of course.'

32

'Good God, you can't pay that!'

'I can. I've got it all together now. It was one hell of a hassle, but I've done it.'

'Look,' I said – I was no lawyer, but I was pretty sure that Dorothy herself might be liable to prosecution, even after all this time and even with the money having been repaid; but it didn't seem to have occurred to her yet, nor for that matter to her blackmailer, so there wasn't a lot of point in adding to her worries – 'why on earth don't you tell John? He knows about the loan – and presumably about the jewellery being entailed?'

Dorothy looked at me for a moment before replying.

'Why not? You know John; he'd never let me give in to blackmail, and then the whole thing would come out. It's all so unfair, if I hadn't married John, or if he hadn't been who he is, none of this would have happened. The Press would never have shown the slightest interest in a scandal concerning an obscure Gloucestershire widow. Why should poor darling George's reputation suffer because of what I do, years after his death? I adore John, I really do, but that doesn't mean that I've got to forget George, does it?' She looked up at me appealingly. 'Well, does it?'

'Of course not,' I said.

'And another thing. How do you think John himself is going to feel if I tell him that I want to spend fifty thousand pounds just to save my first husband's name? I know he's always thought he came second-best with me. It's not true, but he thinks it. That's why he must never know. I can't hurt him like that.'

'Nonetheless, I think I ought to talk to him. Or at least to Julia. . . . '

'Derek, you swore. You can't go back on it now.'

And nothing that I could say would persuade her to release me from that promise. Not the least of my worries was the thought of Dorothy, in what I had now seen for myself to be a very distressed state of mind, wandering about London with all that money on her. I could at least follow her to see that she came to no harm – and I had to be content with that.

She came out of the building into the lamplight, wearing a headscarf, a brown Barbour coat and fawn trousers, and a green canvas bag hung from her right hand. I had been waiting in my car for what remained of the morning and all afternoon and evening – starving. It was just short of 10.30 p.m.

She got into her own car and drove off, and after that it was unexpectedly easy. Through the small residential streets of Westminster I let her get as far ahead as I reasonably could, because the last thing I wanted was to be caught out following her, but I reckoned I needn't have worried. It was all too obvious that she was paying little enough attention to her own driving and she couldn't have had any at all to spare for her rear-view mirror. Left into Victoria Street, where the traffic was fuller and I managed to keep at least one car, usually two, between hers and my own, right at the end, up to Hyde Park Corner where both sets of traffic-lights were with us and on in the direction of Marble Arch. She moved over into the right-hand lane, however, and turned right to cross into Upper Brook Street, on over Bond Street and into Hanover Square. The lights were against her, crossing Oxford Street, and I nearly found myself coming right up behind her, but I managed to pull in behind a parked lorry just in time. The lights changed and we crossed over, into and round Cavendish Square. I had been pretty certain for some time now that her ultimate destination would prove to be somewhere in Regent's Park, although if that were the case I wouldn't have chosen the same route myself, and this became more likely when, reaching Portland Place, she turned left.

I decided that I had better take far closer order now, because I didn't dare to risk being cut off from her by the traffic-lights when we crossed Marylebone Road. Once over, I dropped behind again and, when she turned left into the Outer Circle, I let her get a good hundred yards ahead. It was just as well, because she pulled up suddenly on the right-hand side of the road and I still managed to be sixty yards behind her when I drew in on the left.

I'd remembered at one point during the long afternoon wait that my field-glasses were in the boot of the car and, thinking that they might come in useful, I'd immediately got them out. I picked them up now, from where they lay on the passenger-seat beside me, and focused them. She was double-parked alongside a van which looked about the right size and shape but, from the angle that I was in relation to it, it was impossible to see what, if any, name was painted on the side.

The door opened, and Dorothy got out. She looked hesitantly all around her – luckily I'd already thought to douse my own car-lights – and then she went and tried the doors of the van. She seemed to have a bit of trouble with them at first – fumbling out of sheer nervousness, I supposed – but then she managed it, fetched the canvas bag from her car, put it in, slammed the doors shut, went back to her own car again and drove off. I laid down the field-glasses with a feeling of intense relief that my escort duty was over; she'd be safe enough on her own now, finding her way home.

And then I picked them up again. It honestly hadn't occurred to me up to that moment but, if I myself were to hang around for a bit longer, I might just catch a glimpse of whoever came for the money and thereby be in a position to help nail the blackmailer, should Dorothy ever allow me to do so. I settled down for another wait.

It can't have been more than five minutes, although it seemed much longer, when a man came sauntering round the curve of the railing with a nonchalance that suggested no more than a stroll in the park before bedtime, casually opened the van doors, peered inside and shut them again. A man whose face, as he paused for a moment under the street-light before getting into the front and driving off, I was able with the aid of the field-glasses to identify, beyond all reasonable doubt, as that of Rupert *bloody* Massingham, who not so long ago had appeared, it seemed out of nowhere, to dominate so many of my own personal worlds: politics, the Yardley foxhounds, and . . . Julia, of whom in recent weeks he had been seeing far too much for her own good.

Or, at any rate, for mine.

II

FORRARD AWAY

Wednesday, 22 January to Thursday, 23 January

Julia, already in her dressing-gown, met me in the hall.

Hair, only a micro-shade off being true blonde, swinging freely, thick silky eyebrows, little nose tilted upwards and very slightly sideways at the tip, high cheekbones, high breastline, too – all the attributes that had instantly attracted me to her on our first meeting some years back. Her hands were empty, but there was a distinct aura of hair-curlers and a rolling-pin hovering not very far away.

'Where on earth have *you* been? They told me the House of Lords rose at seven.'

'Sorry. Pratt's,' I said, giving the name of the exclusively masculine club open only in the evening and consisting effectively of two small basement rooms off St James's Street. 'I looked in there for a drink ... and sort of stayed.'

It was the best that I had been able to think up as an alibi on the way home.

'Did you see my father there?'

'No,' I said, truthfully this time.

Her little chin jutted forward, grey-green eyes seething.

'That's funny. He rang up twice from there asking for you, said he'd stay on until eleven o'clock just in case you came in.'

The alibi crumbled into rubble around my feet.

'Look,' I said, 'I can't tell you where I've been or what I've been doing, but I absolutely promise you that it's nothing that you'd disapprove of – quite the contrary.'

Julia didn't reply. She turned and went into the drawing-room, slumped down into an armchair and stared at the empty fireplace.

I followed her in and sat in the one on the other side.

'Hadn't you better ring up Daddy?' she said without looking up.

I glanced at my watch. Nearly midnight. John would be back at their flat by this time. I couldn't speak to him with Dorothy there and, in any case, what had I got to tell him?

'It'll keep till the morning,' I said.

There was a long unhappy silence.

I decided that the time had come to abandon an untenable defensive position and move into the attack.

'I've been hearing things about Rupert Massingham.'

The atmosphere switched dramatically from chill to steam heat.

'Rupert? What things?'

'He's involved in something. I can't tell you what, but it's pretty unsavoury.'

She looked up at me sharply. 'Did you hear of it through politics?'

'No,' I said. That at least was true enough; as far as the political world was concerned, Rupert's reputation was immaculate.

'But you still won't tell me. Why not?'

'I can't. Not without betraying a confidence.'

'You've never liked Rupert. You're jealous of him, that's all.'

'It's not all,' I said lamely, although I had to admit to myself that it was at least a part of it.

'There's no need to be, you know. Can't you see that I just find him good company and amusing to be with? Which is more than I can say for you sometimes.'

It struck me as a trifle ironic that what looked like developing into the worst row we had had yet arose solely from my trying to help out *her* stepmother at the direct request of *her* father.

'I'm sorry,' I said, 'but you'll just have to trust me. I don't want you to see him again.'

'That'll be difficult. I'm having lunch with him tomorrow. I can always keep my eyes glued to my plate, I suppose, if that'll make you any happier.' Julia flounced to her feet. Maddeningly, she never looked more desirable than when she was really angry. 'I really don't see any point in continuing this conversation. I'm going to bed.'

I sat on alone until hunger got the better of me. Out in the kitchen there was a plateful of something that Julia had left in the hot drawer of the oven for me, and I poured out a glass of very strong whisky and water to accompany it. It looked and smelt delicious, but I ate mechanically and without really tasting it. Then I went on drinking whisky until I was sure that I had given her time enough to drop off to sleep – and I followed her up to bed.

I woke early to find the Julia-shaped indentation in the bed beside me empty. An immediate search revealed that she had left the house as well and, in the clear light of morning, I realised that I couldn't entirely blame her. Although I had implied quite a lot, I hadn't been able to tell her a single thing to justify it the night before.

I dressed quickly and drove to the House of Lords.

The room that I was currently occupying there belonged by rights to the Deputy Chief Whip – the Captain of the Yeomen of the Guard, to give him his official title, for all

Lords Whips hold appointments in the Royal Household as well – who had been away ill for some weeks; as next in line among the Lords-in-Waiting, or junior Whips, I was temporarily occupying his place.

I had intended to ring up John Elton immediately on arrival, but as I came through the door the telephone on the desk was ringing already.

It was Dorothy, his wife.

'Derek? It was sweet of you to come round yesterday and listen so sympathetically. I felt so much better after you left.'

'How did it go?' I asked.

'Like clockwork. I found the van parked just where he said it would be, left the money and scarpered. You can't imagine the relief.' She certainly sounded a lot more cheerful.

'Have you got the papers back yet?'

'No, but I wasn't expecting to, quite this early. Don't worry, they'll be along soon, I'm sure of it. Thank you a million times,' she said.

When she had gone, I dialled John Elton's number in the City.

'Sorry about last night, John. By the time I got home it was far too late to telephone.'

'That's all right, old boy. Did you find anything out?'

'Nothing much to report, I'm afraid,' I said contriving to avoid telling a direct lie, 'but I did get the impression that whatever it was that has been worrying Dorothy might be over now.'

'Just what I felt myself when I got back last night – and this morning she was her old self again, thank God. The *last* thing I need is any worries at home just at the moment, Derek. Bless you for what you did.'

I put down the receiver and leant back in my chair. Even as I did so, the warm feeling of temporary euphoria left me. Two satisfied customers. That was fine as far as it went – but what about me?

My own problem was twofold.

First, Julia. How could I possibly stop her making a fool of herself over a man whom I now knew to be a blackmailer – and of her own family at that – when I was totally inhibited by my promise to Dorothy from telling her about it, and when experience had shown that it wasn't even possible for us to discuss him rationally without having a row?

Second, Rupert himself. It was my clear duty as a Whip, understood and accepted by everyone in the political world, if I so much as suspected fallibility in one of my ministerial colleagues, to take instant steps to bring it to the attention of my superiors – and how was I going to do *that* when the same considerations over Dorothy applied?

There was only one consolation that I could see . . . and it was a small one. The two problems, separate and distinct though they were, were interconnected. Solve the second and I would at least have gone part of the way towards solving the first. And the key to both was undoubtedly Rupert. Just exactly what did I know about Sir Rupert Massingham, MP?

The immediate answer was: not very much.

I first remembered hearing his name mentioned as the very good amateur huntsman of a pack of foxhounds somewhere in the West Country. Then, at the last general election, he had stood as Conservative candidate for Halverton, a constituency adjoining the one that I myself lived in, in Northamptonshire. Until then, it had been regarded as a fairly safe Labour seat, but he had won it – against all the odds and, as I subsequently learnt, everybody's expectation but his own.

My own local pack of foxhounds, The Yardley, happened at the time to be needing a new mastership for the following season and, as part of our country lay in his new constituency and was also within relatively easy commuting distance from Westminster, Rupert had immediately applied. It would enable him to go on hunting five days a fortnight. He would hunt hounds himself as one of four Joint Masters – three more were forthcoming from within the county – and, if the Hunt Committee, of which I myself was a member, were satisfied with his first season he would undertake to serve for at least three.

His first season had been an unqualified success and fully justified the reputation that had preceded him. By the first of May he had bought a house in that part of Northamptonshire common to both hunting country and constituency, from which he could nurse the two together, and he had spent the summer getting to know every farmer, landowner and gamekeeper personally. And, from the Opening Meet in November, right through to the time of the Hunt point-to-point in March, he had shown better sport than the Yardley had seen for years.

All this had seemed set to continue for the promised three-season span, or even longer, when at one of the periodic government reshuffles Rupert Massingham had been made a junior minister early the previous July.

Cubhunting had started late last year, well into September, and to begin with he had had to leave some days in the hands of his kennel-huntsman, who was good enough with hounds – although nowhere approaching the same class as Rupert. But, as the season proper had progressed and with it his own political commitments, the minority had gradually become the majority until, after the Christmas Recess, Rupert had only been able to hunt them on the very occasional day. His Joint Masters had loyally 'cleared' the country for him – liaising with farming and shooting interests – and he himself had but to get out of a car at the meet for hounds to leave the man who had been living with them and caring for them, twenty-four hours a day

42

almost, and stream over to Rupert as though he had never been away.

All this meant that I had been seeing little enough of him in the country recently, and even less in London. Our political paths rarely crossed, and of his private life I knew nothing. But I did know someone who could tell me, if anyone could . . . I reached for the telephone again and rang up Jimmy McKay.

Jimmy was a political journalist, or 'Lobby Correspondent' as they are more generally known. Their job, as distinct from 'The Gallery' who deal with the actual proceedings in both Houses of Parliament, is to cover the background to politics by interviewing Members in the lobbies outside. Their ethical standards are higher than any other section of the Press in the country, probably in the world – anything told them by a politician 'on lobby terms' is sacrosanct – but a good Lobby man is expected by his newspaper to be aware of a political story even before it happens. And foremost among these, absorbing the slightest item of news value apparently through his fingertips by a sort of electro-osmosis, was Jimmy McKay.

He was also among the most scrupulous. It was always said of him that, if any politician who had been drinking with him inadvertently let something slip that in a more sober moment he would come to regret, Jimmy's mind possessed a sort of built-in abort mechanism that would erase it completely. He himself drank neat whisky in enormous quantities – which was perhaps not surprising in a Scotsman, but with Jimmy it was invariably Bourbon, which *was* – without any visible effect whatsoever. He worked for the *Guardian*, not usually the favourite daily reading for a Tory Whip in either House; none the less Jimmy McKay had become a great personal friend of mine.

On three separate occasions I had been indebted to him for a luncheon that would have cost the greater part of my own weekly salary. He had once told me that it was a rule of his to entertain politicians at a standard in inverse proportion to their position on the political ladder – it was in his view a waste putting good food and wine in front of a Cabinet minister, who invariably had other things on his mind. And it was this hospitality that it now seemed an ideal opportunity for me, in some small measure, to repay.

I reached him on the telephone at the second attempt.

'Jimmy? Derek Thyrde, here. Look, there's something I want to ask *you* for a change. Are you doing anything for lunch today? Pity. Yes, I realise it's short notice. What about tomorrow? No, this is on me. Shall we say White's, then? Yes, the club, top of St James's on the right. Splendid. See you there tomorrow, then. Twelve forty-five.'

Having taken the whole of the previous day off, the rest of the morning was unusually busy – as I knew the afternoon and evening would be as well. But I did find time to do two small pieces of research. There was no such name as 'Glocksfoot Restorations Ltd' in the London telephone directory but, then, I had hardly expected that there would be. From *Kelly's Street Directory*, the warehouse building appeared to belong to a firm called 'South London Ware-houses', and that wasn't in the telephone book, either.

Then at lunchtime I drove round to have another look at the warehouse itself. I parked the car some fifty yards short of it, walked down to the wooden gates with the faded guard-dog notice on them and looked through the gap as before. There were still no guard dogs, and this time no van, either, with or without the name Glocksfoot on it. The empty yard sloped down to where, at the far end, the wall of the warehouse rose tall and grey and totally unbroken before me. Of any form of opening, or anything that could resemble, or in any way give the impression of being the entrance to a tunnel, there was no sign at all.

'This is indeed an honour, Derek.'

At my suggestion we had gone straight up, taking the right fork at the half-landing of the branched staircase, and into the coffee-room so as to make sure of one of the more secluded tables by the window for luncheon by having our drinks there. A mane of badger-coloured hair the tone and texture of a shaving-brush reached down to his coat-collar, eyebrows to match bristling out from his forehead like bunched antennae, big-boned and tweed-suited, Jimmy McKay somehow contrived to look gaunt and stocky at the same time.

'It's the first time I've penetrated into this core of the Tory establishment,' he said.

Jimmy's habitually half-shut eyes swept round the still sparsely populated room, taking in everything. The central cold table with attendant meats and pies and cheeses; the vista of gleaming white linen – interspersed with the glow of mahogany chairback; vaulted buff-coloured ceiling with its azure blue medallions picked out in gilded laurel leaves; high red portrait-hung walls and marble chimney-pieces, white inlaid with green, at either end. Then back to me again.

'How's Julia?'

'Fine, thanks,' I said, hoping profoundly that I was right. She had not come home the previous evening, but it had happened once or twice before, a gesture of independence, so I was not unduly worried . . . yet.

'Have you got any Cousin Louisa Bourbon?' I asked the wine butler apprehensively. I knew that there was no point in bothering to consult my guest.

'I believe so, m'Lord. We keep it for our American members.' His expression confirmed that my standing had taken a distinct dip in his eyes, and it sank even lower when I asked him to bring the bottle. But it rose again, just a notch or two, when I hurriedly ordered a half-bottle of Château Haut Brion, the club's second-best claret, for myself.

I had been wondering exactly how and at what stage I could best bring up the subject of Rupert Massingham without alerting Jimmy McKay's suspicions. After all, Rupert *was* one of my ministerial colleagues. But when the waitress had brought the main course – Dover sole for him and lamb cutlets for me – and Jimmy had heaped his half-moon side-plate with assorted vegetables from the proffered dishes, he watched in silence while I completed the same operation. Then he gave me the opening I needed.

'Well, Derek, what can I do for you?'

I glanced around me. The neighbouring tables were occupied now but engaged in a satisfactory hum of conversation.

'I really wanted to ask you about Rupert Massingham. What do you make of him?'

'As a person, or as a politician?'

'Both,' I said.

'Ambitious, knows what he wants and goes after it. Never put a foot wrong yet, that I've heard of. The way most of your lot are going just at the moment, you could do with one or two more like him.' His eyelids rose fractionally from their half-shut position, but it was only by a thirty-second of an inch. 'Why do you ask?'

I was prepared for that one. 'He's Master of our local pack of foxhounds,' I said, 'and I'm on the committee. People are always asking me, and I really don't know a thing about him. What's his background, for instance?' Jimmy, I knew, possessed a memory-bank for detail that would have been the envy of most computers.

'Background? Well, his grandfather was Harold Massingham, the engineer. Got his baronetcy in the First World War for inventing the Massingham Bridge.'

'The tank thing?' I vaguely remembered having read about it. The early tanks were unreliable over very rough ground, and this was a steel device they could carry about themselves and the leading tank put in place before it led the others over it. A sort of mini-precursor of the Bailey Bridge.

'That's right. And Rupert's father was an engineer of sorts; not in the same league, of course. Never did anything that anyone's ever heard of. Can't be sure of his name – George, I think.'

'And Rupert himself?' I said.

'Nobody knew very much about him before his surprise win at the last election. Went to Eton – before your time, I suppose . . . ?' I nodded. 'And he got an engineering degree, too, I remember someone telling me, but he didn't stick with it. Made a lot of money in the City during his twenties and thirties. Early forties now, I suppose. A bachelor, but never been any suggestion that he didn't fancy the girls or anything like that. Quite the reverse, I understand.'

I myself was all too well aware of that side of Rupert's character. I thought I'd better change the subject quickly.

'And it was last July he was made a minister?' I said.

'Yes, Parliamentary Secretary to Trade and Industry, the first of the new intake to be brought into the Government. Promoted twice since then. Once to Minister of State when that chap had to resign over the incident in that club in Soho. . . . '

I remembered it well. It had been just about the beginning of the Government's present run of bad luck. There had been a disturbance started by a gang of youths at a particularly undesirable establishment in Hare Street. The minister hadn't even been involved himself, but he'd been called in by the police as a witness. The very fact of his having been there, at that particular place, had been enough to make him resign.

47

'. . . and then, when it all came out about Bobby Digby having that run with Honoria, Rupert stepped into his job as Financial Secretary to the Treasury.'

'It's an ill banana-skin that blows no minister any good,' I said.

Jimmy McKay drained his glass and filled it up again. The level of his bottle of Cousin Louisa had been sinking at the same rate proportionately as my decanted half of claret. I knew from past experience that it would be empty at the exact time that our luncheon came to an end.

'What about the future?' I asked.

There was a slight pause, but the answer when it came was emphatic.

'He'll go far.'

'How far?'

'Oh, to the top . . . eventually, I suppose.'

'Could he take over the leadership from Charles Fortescue?'

'That depends on how long Charlie-boy decides to carry on as Prime Minister. At the moment he says he's determined to lead your party into the next election, and the only possible thing anyone's got against him is his smoking.'

The Prime Minister was known to smoke eighty cigarettes a day with total regularity, a sin that was only exceeded in the eyes of the censorious by the fact that he showed no ill effects from them whatsoever. Photographers and cartoonists took care never to portray him without a cigarette in his hand.

'But if he should decide to go sooner' – Jimmy had paused in thought for a moment – 'there's one or two others I'd back in preference to Rupert.'

That, at any rate, was a relief. 'Such as who?' I said.

Jimmy McKay linked his fingers behind his neck and leant back, tilting his chair in a most un-White's-ian manner. All the indigenous inhabitants had, like me, had such behaviour drummed out of them at the nursery-table. I looked round apprehensively, but nobody seemed to be noticing.

'Well, *your* leader, Patrick Oldfield, put himself out of the running when he went to the Lords the other day; otherwise I'd have said him. As it is . . . Peter White, possibly.'

'Really? I know him, of course, but I've never looked on Peter in quite that light.'

'Don't underestimate him, he's been doing very well as Home Secretary. That's why he's never in the news, and he'd have a lot of support. But there's someone else who's a lot closer to home as far as you're concerned.'

I thought frantically. 'I give up. Who?'

'John Elton.'

'But' – this time I really did sit up – 'he's out of politics.'

'Haven't you heard? You know John's old constituency, Gloucestershire East, is vacant since poor Bobby killed himself on the motorway. Well, the local committee are still looking for a new candidate, and there are very strong rumours that he may be persuaded to stand again.'

'Er. . . . ' I hadn't actually. 'Yes, but to be in the running for PM has anybody ever had to resign like John did and made a comeback to that extent?'

'Perhaps not, but I don't know of anybody who added to his political stature by resigning in quite the same way John Elton did, either. His fall from grace was rather a technicality, you know.'

I did know, perhaps better than anybody, because I myself had been closely involved. Some seven years ago John, who in a weak moment had taken his beloved golden retriever, Maud, with him on a private flight to France, had had to let her out of his Piper Seneca on to the grass for a moment – and at the time of a particularly hysterical rabies scare, too. A photograph had been taken, and this had been used to try to coerce his support for a Bill to legalise cannabis, of which, as Shadow Home Secretary, he had up to then been the leading opponent. In a speech to a crowded House of Commons, he had confessed his lapse, denounced his blackmailers, made known his own retirement from politics and effectively killed the Bill, all at the same time.*

But, if John were able to come back now, bringing with him a fresh mind after so long an absence, he could be just the one person who might see through Rupert Massingham – under whose spell everyone else, even including such an experienced political observer as Jimmy McKay, seemed to have fallen.

'My God, I hope you're right,' I said.

And then we went on to talk of other things. I didn't think it was safe to bring the conversation round to Rupert again. Even now, I couldn't be absolutely sure that I hadn't started Jimmy thinking, although as to whether that would have been a good or a bad thing, taking into account all the circumstances, I still hadn't been able to make up my mind.

And Julia still hadn't returned when I got back to the house in Clapham late that same evening. I went disconsolately to bed, and eventually to sleep.

I woke to a pair of bare arms wrapping themselves round my neck and, at the same time, I felt the smooth warmth of her body snuggling up against me from behind.

'Derek,' she whispered, 'are you awake?' I was by then, fully and glad of it. 'I'm so sorry about two nights ago. I cancelled my lunch with Rupert, went down to Burston instead.' Burston Manor, her father's house in Gloucestershire.

I inched myself about, until my arms were round her, too,

*See *The Man Who Lost His Shadow* (Macmillan, 1979)

and held her tight. And then more loosely, as gradually the doubts and heartache of the past two days became absorbed into a ferment of activity which burnt them out and lapsed at last into a sense of deep contentment. And everything between us, soothed and revitalised, became once more as it had always been.

'I'm glad you came back,' I murmured.

'Had to. Daddy and Dorothy are staying with us at Thyrde tomorrow night. For the Meet the next day, remember.' Suddenly she giggled. 'What did you think Rupert would do? Take advantage of my virginal innocence?'

'What passes for . . . ,' I said.

'Seriously, though, would you rather I didn't come out on Saturday? Rupert's going to be there. He's hunting hounds himself, for once.'

Wrapped as we still were in a warm damp tangle, I felt myself drifting into a blissful sated sleep.

'I wouldn't ask anyone, for *whatever* reason, to give up a day's hunting from Long Mile Goss,' I said.

III

Y'T . . . Y'T . . .

Monday, 27 January to Mid-February

But what turned out to be the run of the season, and as far as I myself was concerned probably the best day's hunting that I had had in my life, did nothing to reconcile me to the perfidy of Rupert – to whose skill as a huntsman it was largely due. It was still my clear duty to bring what knowledge I had, with proof if possible, to the attention of my political superiors. But what could I do?

The immediate answer was nothing. I was still bound by my promise to Dorothy. The last thing I myself wanted was to risk damaging my newly restored, but still precarious, relationship with Julia. And to these was now added a third factor: nothing that I did must be allowed to interfere with the chance of a political comeback for John.

Since Jimmy McKay had first mentioned the possibility of Sir John Elton standing for his old seat again, it had been becoming more and more attractive in my eyes. His political judgement, the loyalty that he could instantly inspire in those around him and, above all, his manifest integrity were badly needed now, even if it hadn't been for the apparently insoluble problem of Rupert.

If he himself realised this, there was no doubt in my mind but that his sense of duty would ensure that he took the right decision. My only reservation was, even if he saw the need, would his own modesty prevent him from seeing himself as the man to fill it? But of one thing I was certain. Once John got an inkling of any sort of scandal that might affect him – even at second hand and, since Dorothy had paid up, however remote the chance of it coming out – nothing would persuade him to risk being the cause of any embarrassment to his political friends, whatever his own inclination might then be.

During the days that followed, the newspapers began to speculate openly, at first on whether, and then increasingly on when, John would allow his name to go forward. There was even mention of his being the logical successor to Charles Fortescue, and this was pursued with enthusiasm by the Tory, and with resigned acceptance by the Labour, press.

As for Julia, she and I continued in an outwardly relaxed and comfortable manner, but I was pretty sure that she was strongly attracted to Rupert Massingham and equally so that she herself was unaware of the extent of it. I gradually came to the conclusion that she would never get him out of her system unless and until she started seeing him again, however dangerous to my interests such a thing might be. But Rupert had become a sort of no-go area between us into which I was reluctant to trespass, even while despising myself for failing to do so. In the end it was she who took the first step.

We were sitting in the drawing-room of the Clapham house late one evening.

'Look, Derek,' she said suddenly, 'Rupert keeps on asking me to lunch and I'm running out of excuses. It's – '

'All right,' I said.

' – getting very embarrassing— ' She broke off. 'What did you say?'

'Go and have lunch with him.'

Julia stared at me. 'Are you sure you don't mind?'

'Not if you don't start falling for him.'

'Oh, there's no danger of anything like that.' She got up. 'I sort of said I'd ring him back.'

And the eagerness with which she hurried out to the telephone in the hall did nothing to restore my peace of mind.

I watched the back of her head as she took the receiver off the wall-fitting to the right of the front door, her fair hair bobbing as she started to talk.

'Rupert? Julia. Yes, I'd love to. Next Tuesday? See you then,' she said.

I drove her to the Peers' Entrance of the House of Lords and took her up the staircase and along the corridors to the Central Lobby, the high octagonal chamber that is common ground between the two Houses of Parliament and a regular meeting-place between the respective members of each and between them and the world outside. Formal-suited figures, some stationary, some scurrying, some single and some in groups, achieved or awaited their various assignations under the paternal gaze of gold-badged doorkeeper and helmeted policeman. But it was the man who stood by himself directly beneath the great chandelier in the middle, acting as a pivot round which the bit-players revolved, who dominated the scene.

Rupert Massingham was something over six feet tall, with a build that indicated a conflict between good living and hard exercise – the latter still just winning; thick brown hair, curly and cut short; the jaw of a pit bull, and eyes like a pair of diamond-tipped drills, in that they tended to sparkle and bore into you at the same time.

Julia walked quickly towards him, and he put a hand on each of her shoulders, leant forward and kissed her cheek.

'Good girl. Perfect timing as usual.' Then he turned to me as though he had only just noticed my presence. 'Derek! Here for the lunch, too, dear?'

I shook my head. 'No, I'm just the guide,' I said.

'Do come. Why not?'

One of Rupert's more maddening characteristics was the way in which he could switch almost in mid-sentence from aloof sarcasm to instant charm. They both stood looking at me. It was a situation in which I knew that I couldn't fail to be in the wrong. If I accepted, it would be because I didn't trust Julia; if I refused, it would be because of my dislike of Rupert. I let personal preference be the deciding factor.

'No, I really can't, thanks,' I said.

They walked off down the corridor to the right, their heads – his dark and hers fair – tilted towards each other in a conversational twosome. It was almost as though I hadn't been there at all. I stood and watched them until they were out of sight.

'Well, Derek?' I glanced sideways. It was Jimmy McKay, his badger-coloured eyebrows still bristling towards the direction that the other two had taken. I wondered what he was making of Julia and Rupert going off together like that – and what he might have read in the expression on my own face. Jimmy was the one person whom I would have been glad to see in almost any other circumstances. Still, it might deflect him from the real cause of my interest in Rupert. I groped for something else to talk about.

'What's the latest about John Elton and Gloucestershire East?' I said.

'I was going to ask *you* that.'

'He never said a word to me and I haven't liked to ask. What does the Lobby think?'

Jimmy narrowed his eyelids. 'Well, it's no secret that John's been longing to get back into active politics. But he'd better make up his mind quickly; there'll never be a better opportunity than now,' he said.

'When's the by-election likely to take place?'

'There's no hard and fast rule as there is with a General Election. In fact there's no statutory obligation to hold a by-election at all. It's up to the House of Commons to take official notice of a vacancy and move that the Speaker issue his warrant to a gentleman called the Clerk of the Crown in Chancery, who in turn issues the writ.'

'And how does that happen?'

'In theory any Member of the House of Commons can set the whole thing in motion, but by convention it's always left to the Chief Whip of the Party the late Member belonged to.'

'So, if the Party really want John back, there's no hurry?'

'Again, in principle that's right. There have been cases in the past where by-elections have been delayed for as much as eight or nine months. But in recent years it's become generally agreed that there should be a strict maximum of three calendar months between the death of the previous Member and the motion for the Writ.'

'How long does that give John in practice, then?'

'Well, nominations have to be in by the eighth sitting day after the issue of the Writ, but it's inconceivable that any Party would give the others a head start by not having their own candidate ready before they move for the Writ. Then there'd have to be a bit of leeway in case John finally turned it down, but they could always have an alternative candidate waiting in the wings, I suppose. Let me see.' Jimmy McKay's eyes were narrow slits now.

'Bobby Digby was killed on the Friday before Christmas; that was the twentieth. It's mid-February now, and that gives John not much beyond mid-March – the nineteenth at the very latest,' he said.

I heard a discreet cough coming from behind me. I turned to find one of the doorkeepers from the Lords end of the Palace standing patiently by.

'Beg pardon, m'Lord. Sir John Elton's in your room and wants to see you urgently,' he said.

He was standing in my borrowed room looking at one of the pictures, a Cecil Aldin print of a whipper-in engaged in holloa-ing a fox away from the covertside. He turned as I shut the door behind me.

John Elton had all Rupert's personality and charm, but there the resemblance ended. A good four inches shorter, although built so much to scale that it was hardly noticeable, sandy-haired and modest, almost self-effacing, where the other was aggressively self-confident – an elderly David to a shepherd-boy Goliath but, if it ever came to it, I would be hard put to it to say who would win.

'Good of you to come so quickly, Derek.'

'That's all right,' I said. Jimmy McKay's expression hadn't altered when we had been interrupted a few minutes before, but I knew that he was thinking as I was, that something would shortly be revealed to me at least about the subject of our recent conversation. Personally, I couldn't wait. 'Have lunch with me here. I think I'll be able to get a table.'

'No, I can't do that, thanks all the same. I've got to be back in the City by two.' He glanced at his watch. 'I'm afraid it's Dorothy again.'

'Oh . . . '

My momentary feeling of disappointment was replaced almost immediately by one of guilt. I had been so sure

57

that Dorothy's problems were over that I had completely stopped worrying about them, except inasmuch as they might affect John's own future. Still, this might at least explain his continued indecision.

'But she seemed perfectly all right last time I saw her. Out hunting. The Long Mile Goss day.'

'That was at least a fortnight ago. It all seemed to start up again soon after and it's been getting progressively worse since. I was wondering— '

'Look,' I said, 'I'll give her a ring. Go and see her again, if necessary. I doubt if I'll find anything out, but it might at least cheer her up.'

'I wish you would, old boy. You had such a good effect last time. And . . . you're so much nearer her age than I am,' he said.

I gave John Elton time to get well clear before dialling Dorothy's number.

'How are things?' I said.

'Derek, how sweet of you to ring. Not very good, I'm afraid.'

'Why, what's happened?'

'Nothing. That's just it. It's well over three weeks now, and I *still* haven't got those papers back. I've half a mind to tell John and put an end to the whole thing.'

'Do you really want to?' I tried to inject into my voice a lack of concern that I was far from feeling. Whatever the result of Dorothy and her first husband's original transgression coming out might have been, the fact that she had been prepared to pay fifty thousand pounds to hush it up would blow it up out of all proportion – and John himself would be the first to see that.

'No, of course I don't. But I can't stand much more of this waiting.'

'Don't worry,' I said. 'He's probably just destroyed the papers, and that'll be the last you'll hear of it. Getting them back to you would just about double the risk of him being found out.'

'Do you really think so?'

'Yes, I do. Look, Dorothy, this is important. Whatever happens, promise me that you won't take any steps, even telling John, without consulting me first.'

'I promise. Oh, Derek, you are a comfort. I feel so much better already,' she said.

Which was more than I felt myself. In spite of what I had said to Dorothy Elton, Rupert was now looking to me like the sort of blackmailer who is all too likely to come back for a second helping. I sat on there for fully ten minutes getting progressively angrier about what he was doing to her, and through her to John, and then I did what I probably ought to have done days before. I went and saw my Chief Whip.

Thomas, Earl of Lavenham, listened in silence, his lanky form crouched over his desk, his gaze never leaving my face until I had finished speaking. Then he uncoiled himself and sat upright.

'Let me get this straight. You say that Rupert Massingham, of all people, is a blackmailer. Yet you have no proof of any kind, you won't tell me who he's been blackmailing, what the blackmail is over, or even how much money is involved. Not even on Whips' terms?'

'I can't, Tom.' I had decided that I was only free to pass on what I had found out for myself and that anything that Dorothy had told me must remain sacrosanct. I was even stretching it by disclosing that the papers unnamed hadn't yet been given back. 'I was only told in the first place on condition that I promised,' I said.

'None the less, you are absolutely certain in your own mind that what you have told me is right?'

I nodded miserably. 'I know it sounds ridiculous. Impossible, even.'

'Oddly enough, I believe you.' Tom Lavenham stood up. 'But you must see that you haven't given me anything like enough for me to be able to take it any further. All I can suggest is that you go and talk to Patrick Oldfield yourself. There's just a chance that you may be able to convince him like you've convinced me.'

'I'll do that.'

He shook his head. 'I don't hold out very much hope for you, I'm afraid. He and Rupert are very close. Rupert was Patrick's PPS for a time when he was Home Secretary, and I'm told that it was Rupert who finally persuaded him to leave the Commons and come up and lead the Lords,' he said.

Later that afternoon, I came through the doors that connected the rooms of Lord Oldfield, Lord President of the Council and Leader of the House of Lords, with those of his Chief Whip. I could still feel the icy coldness of the atmosphere that I had left behind me. Tom looked up from his desk.

'Well?'

'He wouldn't listen to me.'

Tom nodded slowly. 'Don't say I didn't warn you. By the way, can you stand in for me at Home Affairs next Tuesday? It isn't very convenient for me to be up in London that morning.'

I grinned at him. I happened to know that there was a meeting at his local National Hunt racecourse on that particular day.

'I'd be glad to,' I said.

The only two Cabinet committees that I was sometimes called upon to attend – Home Affairs, which has to approve in principle proposed new items of government policy, and Legislation, which has the job of deciding whether, when and how each of them should actually figure in the parliamentary programme – were held in the old Treasury Board Room, off Whitehall.

Completed in the first half of the eighteenth century, its walls, covered in green silk, held portraits of long-dead Chancellors of the Exchequer. At the far end, on a little raised dais of its own, stood a gilded throne where George III used to sit whenever he attended meetings of their Lordships of the Treasury, the last monarch to do so. While, round the table which effectively filled the remainder of the available floor-space, printed place-cards, specifying the name of the office rather than that of its holder, were now arranged with a precedence as meticulous as that in an Edwardian servants' hall.

I sat in my allotted position, so far below the salt that I would have done well to bring my own, and watched the rest of the committee take their seats. Rupert Massingham was among them; he had more right to be there than any of us, representing as he did the Treasury in his capacity of Financial Secretary. The Lord President of the Council, chairman of Home Affairs, was the last to arrive.

Lord Oldfield, austere and humourless, I had always found to be a rather cold personality. He had a scholarly manner, was known to eat sparingly and drink hardly at all, yet in spite of these uncongenial characteristics he was possessed of such a reputation for fairness that he was enormously respected and even liked. There was only one item on the agenda, the Law and Order Bill. He gave a nod to the minister who sat two places away from him on his left.

'Home Secretary?'

I looked at Peter White with particular interest. This was the first time that I had had the opportunity to watch him in action since Jimmy McKay had mentioned him as one of the most likely people to replace Charles Fortescue. Pale-haired with a boyish face, he hardly looked old enough to be a serious contender for the office of Prime Minister, but I happened to know that he was not very far short of Rupert's own age.

'It's not the Bill itself, Lord President, so much as how its passage is likely to be affected by our recent acquisition of USCRODD,' he said.

USCRODD, he explained, or Ultra-Sonic Crowd Dispersal Device to give it its full title, had been developed by the Israelis and constituted a dramatic new aid to dealing with potential civil disorder. It was based on much the same principle as that of a silent dog-whistle, a dog being able to hear a more highly pitched sound than can a human being. The 'cut-off' frequency, above which nothing can actually be heard, is measured in cycles per second or c.p.s. A new-born baby has a cut-off at about 25,000 c.p.s., but this deteriorates throughout its life until it reaches a low of some 6000 c.p.s. in old age. At this point, it would be found difficult to distinguish between 's', 'th' and 'f', as in the words 'sin', 'thin' and 'fin'. The rate of deterioration varies from person to person, of course. He, Peter White, for example, was now able to hear up to about 18,000 c.p.s., while close contemporaries of his had told him that they couldn't hear sound at that level but still *didn't like it*. This was a good illustration of the phenomenon that, at a frequency just above each person's cut-off, he can be affected by a sound although he cannot actually hear it.

The principle behind USCRODD, then, was this. You took a noise that would be distinctly unpleasant to most people, setting their teeth on edge perhaps, like a knife squeaking on a plate – that was an over-simplification, of course, a far more sophisticated mixture of sounds was in fact used – and transmitted it at frequencies progressing downwards in the 12,000–20,000 c.p.s. waveband, thereby achieving the same ultra-sonic effect on all people in age groups sixteen to sixty. This manifested itself simply in a compulsion to move as far away from the source of the unheard transmission as possible, all thought of rioting forgotten and without knowing why. The youngest, who accordingly would have the sharpest hearing, would be the first to move and, as the appreciation of sound intensity falls off as the inverse square of the distance from the source – that is to say, you double the distance and the sound-level falls to a quarter, treble it and it falls by a factor of nine – would be out of range before the frequency became one which was low enough for them actually to hear. And, as the frequencies became progressively lower, these would be followed by the rest in approximate order of age.

The great advantage of the device was that, as far as anyone had yet been able to find out, it had no harmful side-effects. The compulsion to disperse fell a long way short of panic, and it would never be used at an intensity approaching that of pain level, which might otherwise present a risk to those with weak hearts. It would make virtually obsolete the existing and less satisfactory methods available to the police, such as baton rounds, water-cannon and CS gas. It had never been needed more than it was at this moment when the state of the economy together with unemployment – he glanced apologetically at Rupert and the other minister concerned – had led to unprecedented disorder, and it could make football hooliganism a thing of the past.

The disadvantage, Peter White went on, was this. USC-RODD had been used to great effect in South Africa and this, as colleagues would be aware, had tainted it in the eyes of some people. Not only that, but it had been used there to disperse gatherings that would have been regarded

63

in this country as perfectly legitimate expressions of political opinion. Jonathon Finchley, the Labour spokesman on Home Affairs, had been to see him. In the eyes of his party, he had said, USCRODD taken in conjunction with the wide-ranging measures proposed in the Law and Order Bill would give altogether too much power to the police. He had told him quite frankly that, while he realised that no legislation was needed to issue the police with this new device, it would be more than his job was worth not to do everything in his power to block the Bill unless certain concessions regarding the device were forthcoming.

'The trouble is it's almost too good. Some of the Labour Party are genuinely afraid that it could be the first step towards our becoming a police state.'

The Lord President raised his eyebrows. 'What concessions is he asking for?'

'Just one, really. He wants an undertaking from the Government that it won't be used in connection with anti-nuclear demonstrations. As you know, there are some big ones planned up at Mathersdon for next month. He argues that they are by definition non-violent, and it's true that they'd lose the support of some of their more woolly-minded do-gooders if they ever became otherwise. But he really wants it to be used as a yardstick to cover other peaceful demonstrations which would otherwise be difficult to define. He wants the undertaking in writing, Lord President, and subject to the agreement of this committee I propose to give it.'

'You've consulted the Secretary of State for Defence of course?'

'Yes, and he agrees – albeit reluctantly. He couldn't be here today, but I believe he's represented.'

The earnest young bespectacled junior minister beside me craned forward.

'Parliamentary Under-Secretary of State, Defence?'

'That is correct, Lord President.'

Lord Oldfield glanced round the table. 'Secretary of State for Scotland?'

'The Bill itself doesn't extend to Scotland, but I agree with the proposal.'

'Wales?'

'Agreed, Lord President.'

'Minister of State, Northern Ireland?'

'Yes, Lord President. We've used USCRODD on an experimental basis already, and it would be impossible to overstate its value.'

'Secretary of State for Education?'

'Agreed.'

'Secretary of State for Employment?' Lord Oldfield cast a disapproving glance to where the smoke of that functionary's habitual cigarette wreathed its way upwards until it was lost in the dead white of the ornately moulded sugar-icing ceiling. A look that I doubted whether even he would have dared to direct towards the Prime Minister, a far greater offender in this respect.

'It'll certainly help with the unions. They want picketing to be exempted, too, but I think they'll settle for nuclear demonstrations being taken as a yardstick.'

'Lord Privy Seal?'

The Leader of the House of Commons, whose alternative title that was, nodded. 'I doubt if we'll get the Bill through without it,' he said.

'Chief Whip?'

The man who was Tom Lavenham's opposite number in the Commons remained in silent thought for a moment. Then: 'We'll have a certain amount of difficulty with our own right-wingers of course, but I agree.'

'Lord Chancellor?'

'I don't see how we can do otherwise, but I would like to ask one question. The Home Secretary told us that the device was based on an ultra-sonic transmission. Would it not be possible to avoid its effect by the use of ear-plugs?'

'Home Secretary?'

'To a certain extent, Lord President; in fact the police themselves will be equipped with insulating helmets. But what we are seeking to prevent is a whole crowd suddenly becoming uncontrollable, whether due to incitement or not, and a few agitators who have made themselves immune in some way would be comparatively easy to deal with on their own.'

'Thank you,' the Lord Chancellor said.

'Financial Secretary to the Treasury?'

'I'm sorry to be the only one to introduce a dissentient note into the proceedings, Lord President, but I do see some danger in the course that the Home Secretary is advocating.'

Rupert Massingham spoke in a quiet measured voice, but his eyes seemed to dominate the rest of the table.

'I do, of course, appreciate the necessity of avoiding the use of this machine on genuinely peaceful demonstrations, but there have been isolated instances of violence connected with the anti-nuclear movement in the past. More recently, they have shown themselves willing to break the law in respect of damage to property, and who can say that this may not escalate to violence to the person in the future? Then there's always the possibility of outside agitators who have nothing to do with the movement itself coming in, just the sort of troublemakers that the Home Secretary envisaged in his answer to the Lord Chancellor.'

He paused to take a sip of water, which I judged to be more for effect than for refreshment.

'But my main concern is this. If we do go down this road, just how long is such an undertaking to be deemed to last? Will it only bind the Government for the remainder of this Parliament, for instance, or would it be taken to extend beyond? Perhaps even to a future Conservative administration, after a period in opposition?'

Lord Oldfield looked round the table questioningly.

I raised my hand slightly and caught his eye. Junior Whips in the Lords are not even expected to have an opinion on policy, let alone express one, but I was damned if I was going to be the only person there not to speak.

'I agree with the Financial Secretary, Lord President,' I said.

I did, too. I thought that with the Government's present record of accident-proneness we would be absolutely mad to give an undertaking that in certain circumstances might have to be broken, however remote such a possibility might be. But it was a matter of feeling rather than of reason, and I couldn't have substantiated it.

'I see.' Lord Oldfield's expression revealed that I had sunk even lower in his eyes. Not only had I had the temerity to make unwarrantable accusations against the sainted Rupert, but here I was actually seeking to curry favour with him. He glanced apologetically towards him. 'I'm afraid that the feeling of the meeting's against you, Financial Secretary. I shall have to report that "In the opinion of this Committee," ' he spoke slowly so that the officials on his right could take down the words as he spoke them, ' "with one ... er, two ... dissensions, the Home Secretary's proposal should be agreed to. That is— " '

'Just a moment.' It was the Lord Chancellor who spoke. 'I think that the Financial Secretary has a point. This Committee really cannot commit a future Conservative administration, and I think that it should be made absolutely clear in the report. After all, this device may exist long after the provisions of the Bill have been superseded.'

There were murmurs of assent around the table.

The Home Secretary coughed. 'If it would help the Committee, Jonathon Finchley really is very sympathetic and I think he would accept it if I made it a personal undertaking to him in private, without implicating the Government as a whole. And perhaps' – he looked reproachfully at Rupert – 'only so long as I myself am occupying my *present* office.'

He was clearly shaken that his judgement should have been called into question by Rupert Massingham of all people, one of whose many admirers he must have been.

'That's very generous of you, Home Secretary.' Lord Oldfield looked quickly round the table again. 'Is that agreed, then? Thank you very much,' he said.

I waited for Rupert outside the Treasury Board Room. During the past few days I had been thinking frantically, and the only possibility that had occurred to me was that, if I were to drop a hint to him about what I knew, it might just stop him from trying to extort yet more money from Dorothy. Maddeningly, he was the last to leave.

'Can I have a word with you, Rupert?'

'Not now, dear.' And he went striding on past.

'It's about a firm called Glocksfoot Restorations Ltd,' I called after him.

He turned slowly and walked back, but his expression showed no more than polite interest.

'What of it?'

'How about blackmail?' I said lamely.

'Blackmail, my dear Derek, only happens to people who have got something to hide in the first place. Now, I really must go. Shall I see you out hunting on Saturday?'

'No,' I said. 'I've only got one horse and I'm saving him for the point-to-point in a couple of weeks' time.'

In a convivial moment late one night at a Yardley Hunt party, long before I had had any cause to distrust Rupert or even dislike him, he and I had made a pact to enter our respective hunters for the Members' Race.

He raised his eyebrows. 'Are you still going? I was sure you'd think better of it in the morning.'

'Of course I am. Are *you*?'

'Nothing would stop me,' he said.

IV

YONDER HE GOES

Saturday, 1 March

It was 11.50 a.m., and I was alone in the changing-tent. I
wished I knew where the others were. I had been advised
to have a big breakfast before starting out. I wished I
hadn't. I needed a drink. I didn't want a drink. I wished I
was somewhere else. I wished I was some*one* else. I wished
I knew what I wished. The day of the point-to-point had
arrived.

Just as steeplechases are said to have had their origin
in an eighteenth-century party of foxhunters disconsolate
at the end of a blank day seeking to enliven their journey
home with an impromptu race across country to a church
steeple on the skyline, so point-to-points, their amateur
equivalent, started by being held in a straight line too, literally from one point to another. Both, however, have long
since evolved into broadly oval shapes, point-to-points still
being held over normal farming land but incorporating a
permanent grass track with purpose-built birch fences. And
of these, from the point of view of rider and spectator alike,
the Yardley Hunt's Croombe Ashby course was acknowledged to be among the best in the country.

Situated on two opposing slopes, the paddock, tents,
bookmakers' stands and carpark were on the one and the

bulk of the course itself on the other. Suffering as I do from perennial train fever, I had got there at 10 a.m. – ridiculously early. I was to walk the course at 10.30; and Fred Beamish, the friend with whom I kept my hunter at livery and who over the past weeks had assumed the more exacting rôle of trainer, was to come with me. He had been twenty minutes late.

The course ran clockwise and consisted of nine fences, eight plain and one open ditch, each race being just over two complete circuits, making three and a half miles and nineteen jumps in all. The Start was at the right-hand end of the bottom straight which had two plain fences on it, with the winning-post approximately halfway between them, so the first fence was the only one that was jumped three times.

It was a bitterly cold day – well above freezing-point, but the spasmodic appearances of a watery sun did little to mitigate the effect of the east wind. I had huddled myself into my covert-coat, trying tortoise-like to retract my neck and head into it, as I had walked round memorising the course like a schoolboy; taking note of patches of soft ground to avoid, selecting the best take-off point at each fence and planning my route accordingly. Fred, who may have done a grand job over my horse – I myself had spent one morning at Newmarket under his supervision, galloping Asquith over fences – had been precious little help here.

'You'll have to ride your own race. I can't do it for you,' he had said.

After the second fence, there was a bend to the right and the third and fourth fences were jumped uphill. Then another bend and into the fifth – the first of three along the top straight. Between this and the next there were two barns set roughly at right angles to each other on the inside of the course, which meant that there was a length of at

71

least twenty yards that was out of sight of the spectators anywhere on the opposite hill. '*It all happens behind the barns,*' they used to say, hinting at nameless forms of skulduggery that could be inflicted by one rider on another.

The next fence was the sixth, the only open ditch, guarded at the take-off side by an eighteen-inch rail of grey wood painted yellow at its rounded top. I went up and peered into it, to find that it was merely simulated by a yard of bare earth, but it didn't make it any less menacing with its solid wall of birch twigs, lined to half its height with evergreen, beyond. After that was another plain fence, an 'island' one this time, set rather incongruously by itself in the middle of a field with no hedgerow to justify it, and this was followed by the third right-hand bend and the eighth and ninth fences which were jumped downhill. Finally, back into the bottom straight, past the Start and on to the first fence again, which now became the tenth and would be the last, or nineteenth, next time round.

Fred Beamish had left me at this point in order to 'declare' my horse, confirming it as a certain runner – for this one day only, I had reverted to his former name and entered him as Wait-and-See – while I had gone off to the changing-tent, trying desperately to remember what I had learnt from my walk round the course. I had sat about in my ordinary clothes for as long as I dared and then I had changed into my grandfather's old colours, white nylon breeches and the paper-thin boots that I had borrowed, and sat about in them. The Members' Race, the only one open to hunters like mine that couldn't be registered as thoroughbreds, was first on the card at 12.30. Where on earth was everybody? I looked at my watch again: 12.03, and we had to be weighed out by 12.15!

Suddenly there was a commotion at the door of the tent, accompanied by a snatch of conversation – 'No, that was at

72

Towcester. Fell at the second, Haydock Park, remember' –
and they all came bustling in, dropping their canvas holdalls
on the ground and nodding cheerfully to me as they did
so. There were three of them, two semi-professionals that
I knew well by sight from around the local point-to-point
circuit, but not out hunting – they must have done their
qualifying on weekdays – and Rupert. One of the others
had his false teeth out already and was wrapping them
carefully in a large white handkerchief. I caught his eye,
and he winked at me. Then there was a throwing of boots
about, dropping of coats and shirts, and they all seemed to
be changing in about a tenth of the time that I had taken
to do so.

Rupert looked up from pulling on his first boot.

'You weighed out yet, Derek?'

I shook my head, and he nodded towards the opening
that led into the next partition. 'On you go, dear. We'll be
right behind you.'

I picked up my kit and went through, where I put
my whip and regulation helmet down on the ground and,
holding only the suede racing-saddle with its ridiculous-
looking little aluminium irons, borrowed like the boots,
sat down to be weighed. I was delighted to be told by
the Clerk of the Scales that I was within the 12.7 weight
with a couple of pounds to spare. I carried away the thin
leather weight-cloth with its compensating bits of lead in
it, pressed to my chest like a hard-earned badge of merit
for this achievement, and by this time the other three had
indeed arrived. The two semi-professionals were exactly
the right weight, whereas Rupert, who was the last to be
weighed, was four pounds over.

'Damn, I could have sworn I'd made it,' he said.

Then the bell went. 'Jockeys out!'

I walked out into one of the fleeting moments of sunshine and towards the paddock where the four horses were

73

already being led round, a chestnut in front, then a grey, followed by my horse, Wait-and-See, and finally Rupert's, another bay of much the same size and make but, from his looks, with quite a bit more blood in him.

'Have a good ride, m'lord.'

I stopped and turned, to see a wiry little man in a tweed coat of brown and yellow checks, a bookie's floorman who had become rather a friend of mine because, when there was no racing locally, he liked nothing better than to come out for a day with the Yardley, covering miles on foot and seeing a lot more of hounds in the process than did many of the people on horses.

'Thanks, Syd. What are the odds?'

'The grey's Ear-'ole and the chestnut's Bottle.'

'What's that to us mere mortals?'

The little man grinned. 'Six-to-four and two-to-one. They say the chestnut's the better 'orse if he stands up, but 'e don't always.'

'What about Rupert and me?'

'Sir Rupert's a 'undred-to-thirty – Burlington Bertie. Sorry, squire, you're On the Shoulders – nine-to-two.'

'That's all right,' I said. 'Rupert rides a lot better than I ever will and he's got four or five horses to choose from.' Also, I knew that Rupert had point-to-pointed before, whereas I hadn't. None the less, I had a sudden moment of bravado. 'Put ten quid on for me, will you?'

'My bloke's making a separate book on you and Sir Roop. 'E's Shoulder-on – that's four-to-seven – and you're Wrist – five-to-four.'

'You'd better put my tenner on that,' I said.

I gave my saddle to Fred Beamish and went over to join Julia, where she was standing in the middle of the paddock. 'Good luck, darling. Be careful,' and she gave me a perfunctory kiss on the cheek. Then 'Good luck, Rupert,' she called as the latter strode past, her attention instantly

74

diverted to him. There didn't seem to be very much more at that moment to say.

There was another bell, and I saw that the horses had stopped. Fred Beamish had Wait-and-See's rug off and was tightening the girth and surcingle and pulling down the stirrup-irons. Then he turned and looked expectantly towards me.

As I walked towards him, *suddenly the whole world changed and everything took on a dream-like quality, a feeling of total unreality. Croombe Ashby had become a stage on which there were only four players and I was one of them. Without realising how I had got there, I was up on my horse and parading round with the others. The inside of the chestnut paling was lined with banners advertising local country enterprises above them a blur of faces a medley of indecipherable conversations as I passed by trying to cope with this new existence. My stirrup-leathers were terrifyingly short, and instead of holding my reins with the spare swinging in a loop I had instinctively 'bridged' them, as I had recently been taught to do, into a circle over the withers of this changeling between my knees – gone was the wise old hunter from the covertside, and in his place this arching, prancing, bouncing handful of horse. And then the kennel-huntsman blew his horn and led us out, weaving his way between groups of surging spectators, and down towards the Start.*

There were shouts of encouragement from indiscernible figures as I passed them, and I could hear a loudspeaker blaring at one point, although as to what it was saying I was totally unaware. The first fence was no more than a low menacing smudge of dark to the left of us until, arrived at our destination, the four of us turned and cantered back to have a closer look at it. I can't say that I was very enthusiastic about the idea myself, but it seemed to be the thing to do.

Then we were back at the Start again. The Starter's Assistant fiddled about with my horse's girth and seemed to be satisfied. Then the Starter himself, his flag held downwards, called out the names. 'Smithkin?' 'Yes, sir.' 'Rogers?' 'Yes, sir.' 'Massingham?' 'Yes.' 'Thyrde?' No answer to that one. 'Thyrde?' 'Sorry, yes,' I heard myself saying.

He held his flag up. A hundred yards down the course towards the first fence, the Starter's Assistant, who seemed miraculously to have transported himself there, did the same. 'Form a line and walk up.' I was at the left of it, Rupert next to me. 'No, I said walk. Right, go on.' There was a flash of white moving downwards, reflected instantly by the Assistant's own flag a hundred yards ahead, 'Poop, poop, poop,' went the horn . . . and then we were racing and it all became real again.

Every scrap of nerves had gone now, to be replaced by an unbelievable undreamt-of sense of exhilaration, the wind in my face, the rhythm of hoofbeats, yanking of bits and jostle of competing horses. Cold was a thing of the past, and there was the Starter's Assistant, scuttling aside to safety, and beyond him the first fence. It was menacing no longer, but wide, inviting, comfortable – would it have been so had there been ten or more horses? – and then we were over, line abreast the four of us, taken at the gallop from a full stride before and landing more than a full stride ahead.

I was elated at my own performance. Wait-and-See was a racehorse just like the rest of them. I was conscious of the crowds to the left of us, jumble of faces, sharpness of voices; vanity took over, and I leant lower over the horse's shoulders thrusting my feet forward to look the part. Then I saw the second fence looming.

It was narrower, this one, and a passing glimpse of a couple of St John's men with a stretcher at their feet beside it made the elation dissipate slightly, allowing a feeling of mortality to creep in. But we still took it four abreast, the chestnut on the inside, then the grey, then Rupert, then me, and we were up and over. And there was the first bend ahead of us, marked by three flags, red-painted wood on

76

high white poles, a sheep-hurdle to the right of each of them.

The chestnut edged ahead as we turned uphill, Rupert keeping level with the grey, and I would have liked to kick on here to keep level with him, too, as we approached the third. But I had taken taken note of a patch of very soft going on the take-off side in front of me and I was too close to Rupert to tuck in behind him, so I imperceptibly tightened the reins to ease my own horse, for fear he might flounder and perhaps pull a tendon. It was no easy matter, but the hill was there to help me. Wait-and-See took it at a good half-gallop and then we, too, were over.

The others had surged away from me, and I thought that I had probably lost contact for good, but I pressed my thumbs into my horse's neck to wake him up a bit, managing to maintain the distance, and there was the fourth fence, still an uphill one. Wait-and-See jumped this one superbly, gaining a length or two on Rupert, and straight ahead was the dark mass of Ashby Fox, reckoned to be the second-best covert to Long Mile Gorse in the whole of the Yardley country.

There was another line of flags just short of it, and we rounded the bend into the top straight. The grey was up with the chestnut as we did so, Rupert tucked in behind the grey and I behind Rupert – and we jumped the fifth fence in that order. I was gaining steadily on Rupert and I'd almost caught up with him by the time that the barns flashed by to the right of us. *It all happens behind the barns.* But nothing did.

The grey and the chestnut were a couple of lengths ahead of us as we came to the open ditch for the first time. I tightened down into my horse and kicked on, and I had a brief impression of the three Hunt Terrier-men, the fence-stewards for this particular fence, standing in line as they always did with their battered old land-rover behind them. 'Go on, m'Lord,' shouted Tom on the right and Ted on the left in unison, as Rupert and I left the ground together, and I was struck with a flash of pleasure not unmixed with surprise that it was me rather than him that they were rooting for – and then we were over. Cully, in the middle, had remained silent as usual but he had been smiling as I had momentarily caught his eye.

We approached the seventh – the island fence – in the same order, the chestnut and the grey taking off together, Rupert behind the grey, and I to his left. 'Hold up, you stupid sod,' he bellowed, and I heard the thwack of his whip on his horse's flank and then a crash as he hit the top of the fence. I was certain he'd be unseated, but as I rounded the bend to go downhill I turned my head as much as I dared without losing balance and there he still was firmly back in the saddle again. Even so, he had lost a number of lengths. I eased over to my right so as to take advantage of the bends – there was everything to play for now; here at last was one way of putting at least a minor break into Rupert's relentless run of success.

The chestnut was a good length ahead of the grey now, but I noticed that the latter still kept his place just to the left, no doubt because of the chestnut's falling record, so I decided to follow his example and, as we jumped the first fence downhill, I tucked in behind the grey instead. Approaching the ninth, the grey did pull over behind the chestnut – I knew that the bend into the bottom straight was only a yard or two beyond the fence and an extremely sharp one at that, and perhaps the risk of losing too much ground was even greater here than that of being brought down, and again I followed his example. And then we were all over, round and past the start, and there was the first fence again, now the tenth, wide and welcoming ahead.

The grey pulled out and drew level with the chestnut, and I did the same with the grey and we jumped it almost together. Past the crowds again where the finish would be next time round, again the preening and adjusting of the seat to look the part, into the narrower eleventh, little to choose between us, and as I inched up level with the other two I began to feel a tiny touch of hope within me – could I really stand a chance of winning the whole race? – perhaps I should have put my tenner on the main book after all – and always the exhilaration, the sound of the hoofbeats and the wind in my face.

Round the bend, and the chestnut, having the advantage of it, gained on the grey again and I moved over to behind the grey so as to avoid that patch of soft going altogether when we took the first fence uphill again, now the twelfth. All safely over. Then I noticed a nod being exchanged between the other two and, silently, horribly, deliberately, they seemed to take off and surge away from me. One moment they were there, the next not. So much for my presumption of thirty seconds or so before. When I cleared the twelfth and saw the blurred brown outline of Ashby Fox silhouetted at the top of the hill again, there were the other two disappearing round the bend into the top straight and, when I, too, was rounding it, they were out of sight altogether. Wait-and-See, that up-and-coming new star of the point-to-point world, had evaporated like steam from his sweat-sodden flanks, and all that I had between my knees was a tired old hunter called Asquith again.

I had a sudden feeling of total aloneness, but I glanced behind me and there was Rupert taking far closer order now. He was gaining on me as we went into the fourteenth, and there were the barns on the right again and that blind twenty-yard stretch. *It all happens behind the barns.* I sensed that he was upsides with me even before I heard the grimness in his voice, 'Move over, dear,' and felt the pressure of Rupert's boot against mine, his horse's head boring against

Asquith's, riding us off the grass track relentlessly towards the right. Then the pressure was released as we came out into general view again and, approaching the open ditch at full gallop as we were, I was fighting with my left rein to regain my course.

I realised afterwards that I ought to have kept on in the direction towards which I had been diverted, thereby leaving the wing of the fence harmlessly on my left. But that would have meant taking an instantaneous decision, and the instinct to remain in the race had been too strong for me. I grappled with that left rein with the strength that only comes from desperation and I'd have made it, too. But, just as we were on the point of jumping, there was a flash of white, and Rupert, who was now level with Asquith's head, pulled something like an enormous handkerchief out of the top of his breeches causing him to shy off to the right again. The high birch wing, at its thickest and strongest where it joined the main fence, seemed to rise before me until we met it in a rending, splintering, crash and, for what seemed like seconds, I was falling, falling, falling. The thud as I hit the ground came, almost as an anticlimax, from a long way away.

My immediate impression was that I was dying – and very noisily, too. I was lying on my back letting out great heaving sobs, literally fighting for breath for what seemed like an age but it must have been less than a minute. And then I was able to focus again and I became aware of Cully's wise smile-wrinkled face hovering solicitously over me.

'You lie still, me duck. You'm winded, that's all.' It was Tom on the right who spoke. I hadn't any option. Cully was holding my left shoulder firmly down to the ground with one hand while he checked my arms and legs for breakages with the other.

'Don't you fret about Asquith, m'Lord, he'm all right. Try if you can move your fingers.' Ted, on the left, had one arm held imperiously out sideways, keeping at bay two indignant-looking young St John's men, whose prerogative it should rightly have been. 'Now your toes.'

Tall, dark-haired and cadaverous, they weren't twins, although anyone might have been forgiven for mistaking them for such. Ten years older, stocky and a good head shorter, Cully was the undoubted brains of the operation. They had been Hunt Terrier-men to the Yardley for more years than I could remember.

I could hear distant cheering from the direction of the winning-post – the favourite by the sound of it – as they helped me to my feet.

Ted was holding the piece of white linen, plainly more than a handkerchief, which he must have picked up from the top of the fence where Rupert had let it fall, and he looked down at it now with an air of mild perplexity.

'Now, what are he done that for?' he said. 'Ought to be looked into, that did.'

'Looked into?' Tom's voice was scornful. 'Ought to be warned off, more like. We seen what that Massingham done to you, Derek. You come along of us to the Stewards.' He spoke with a venom that surprised me. Never before had I known any of the three have an unkind thought in his head.

'No, wait a minute,' I said. I was thinking very fast. Would the Stewards be likely to believe such an accusation, even with the evidence of the piece of linen and even if it was supported by official observers, against the highly respected Master of the very Hunt whose point-to-point this was? My immediate boss, the Lord President of the Council, I happened to know, disapproved of hunting and its by-products, although he was far too fair a man to seek to inflict his non-political views on his subordinates, and, even if I were successful in showing up Rupert over such a matter, where would that get me? Above all, where would it leave me with Julia? But here at last were three people who didn't seem to subscribe to the general adulation for Rupert and who just might prove to be useful allies in the future.

'Look,' I said, 'I'm pretty sure that Rupert's mixed up in something infinitely nastier than a bit of dirty riding and I don't want to do anything that might prejudice my getting him for that. If the time should come when I need any help, can I get in touch with you?'

Tom looked at Cully who, after a momentary pause, nodded. 'You do that, Derek. Ted'll run you back in the jeep, and me and Cully'll stay and look after the fence.'

Jess, the matriarch of the terrier clan, grey about the muzzle and ears and the only one privileged to be present on such non-operational occasions as this, was occupying the front passenger-seat of the land-rover and was bundled unceremoniously into the back by Ted. Installed in her place, I was rattled back round the outside of the course in a way that pinpointed every bruise in my body.

I was met by an anxious-looking Julia.

'How's Asquith?' I asked.

'Seems to be feeling his off-fore a bit, but Fred says he'll be OK. How are *you*? That's more the point.'

'Fine, thanks.'

'Poor old Derek.' Then her eyes shone. 'But isn't it wonderful about Rupert?'

'Wonderful?'

'Haven't you heard? The chestnut fell at that fence before the sharp turn into the straight, brought down the grey, and Rupert won. Come on, he's opening some champagne in the Masters' tent and wants us to be there.'

One look at the eagerness in her face instantly dispelled any idea I might have had about telling her what Rupert had tried to do to me. But it didn't make me feel any happier about it.

'I don't think I will, thanks.'

Her smile vanished. 'Look, Derek, I know you don't like Rupert, but if you don't come everyone will think you're being unsporting.' The tone of her voice told me that she would, even if nobody else did.

'Oh, all right. But the rules say you have to see the doctor after a fall. I'll join you there,' I said.

In the Masters' tent, everyone was thronging noisily round Rupert Massingham. Julia turned as I came up to them.

'How did you get on with the doctor?'

'All right, thanks. He asked me a lot of damn fool questions, such as what was my name and what day it was. He thinks I'm relatively sane still.'

Rupert, beside her, was holding an enormous Victorian silver cup, with foxes' masks forming handles on either side.

'Congratulations,' I said, trying to assume as pleasant an expression as was consistent with glaring into those eyes of his at the same time.

'Derek, my dear chap, what bad luck it was your falling like that. I'm sure you'd have beaten me.'

He held his trophy up and out towards me. It was full to the brim with what must have been at least a magnum and I took as small a sip out of it as politeness allowed, still keeping my eyes riveted on his over the top of it as I did so. I never did care much for champagne, especially when drunk out of a communal bucket – to say nothing of an ill–gotten one.

Then I went over and poured myself out some whisky at the bar.

All the attention and chatter of the throng was focused on Rupert again. There was a very pretty redhead looking rather neglected on the fringe of it, and I toyed with the idea of going over and talking to her but almost immediately I dismissed it. It would be giving far too much of an excuse to Julia and Rupert – if it ever occurred to them that they needed one, that is.

I had another glass of whisky, standing where I was by myself. Followed by a third. Then I went out into the cold air, back to the changing-tent and got into my ordinary clothes again.

The front row of the carpark, nearest to the finishing straight, consisted of a line of about a hundred numbered reserved places, and I always made a point of walking down the length of it at least once during a Croombe Ashby point-to-point afternoon. It was a hazardous proceeding at the best of times, because every boot held its full quota of bottles and at least three-quarters of the occupants were personal friends of mine. I started with the car opposite the first fence, at the extreme right-hand end of the line.

'Hard luck, Derek. What'll you have – whisky?'

'Yes, please,' I said.

'Come on down to us next, m'lord.' A bottle of Bells held in the air was being used to beckon me towards the Range-Rover two along the line.

'Whisky for you, Derek? We've got a bottle of malt somewhere, or do you prefer the cooking?'

'Here you are, m'lord, poured out for you already.'

'Sorry, we're out of Scotch. Gin and Martini. Do you good for a change.'

'Whisky. . . . '

'Sloe gin. . . . '

'Whisky. . . . '

'Cherry brandy. . . . '

'Whisss. . . . ' Suddenly, without the least bit of warning the bookmakers' boards, nine or ten of them at the top of the hill, started flickering against the skyline. I was perfectly all right, my mind was brilliantly sharp and clear, it was the Croombe Ashby course that was spinning, and its gyrations seemed to be affecting my word-forming processes, too. I had had nothing to eat since that appalling breakfast – I hadn't even got down the line as far as my own car yet – and it was certainly far too late to begin eating now. There was nothing for it but a rapid walk round the course again until I regained my equilibrium.

Mumbling an apology to my latest set of hosts, I left them and started out.

Past the winning-post, no cheers of encouragement now but, then, not a lot of preening and adjusting, either.

Past the second fence. Did I really jump that? TWICE!

There was the first bend, the three flags marking it, each with its attendant sheep-hurdle. Jump one of those on foot, shouldn't wonder. Wiser not to try, perhaps.

There was a drumming of distant hoofbeats from some-where behind me. Better get off the course, then. Off the course? Here was confusion, the word 'course' not only applies to the whole area on which the point-to-point is held, spectators, carpark, paddock, tent, bookies and all, it also applies to the actual grass track with fences on it along which the competitors race – 'course, course!' – it all seemed too difficult at this stage in the afternoon. I stumbled over to safety beyond the hurdles as some fifteen or twenty horses and riders kaleidoscoped by.

Up the hill to the third fence, passing on the inside well away from that patch of very soft going – for fear I might flounder, and perhaps pull a tendon – past the fourth fence and on to Ashby Fox – many was the good hunt I'd had from there, all grass, all jumpable fences . . . not those on the course, of course – 'course, of course!' – they were sacrosanct and in any case guarded from the weather by metal sheeting except on this actual day.

Round the bend at the top, there ahead was the fence before the open ditch and beyond it would be the stretch that was hidden behind the barns – *it all happens behind the barns* – hey, that was odd: the fence before the open ditch really would have had a ditch in front of it in the normal course of events, had it not been channelled under the course in a culvert – 'course of events, under the course!'

There wasn't a lot of water in it, mainly mud and quite a lot of that. It was deep, too, and just too wide to step across. Easy enough to jump, though – better take a run at it – one, two, three paces back – turn – three, two, one, jump – slither, teeter – SPLASH!

By God, it was wet and, by God, it was cold. I was lying on my back gazing helplessly up at the sky above me, incapable of movement, cast like a heavy ewe in springtime. Whether or not I'd have puffed up and eventually exploded in quite the same way, I wasn't to discover. I was rescued by two smirking St John's men hauling me ignominiously out and on to my feet, one to each hand, avenging had they known it the slight inflicted on their confrères at the next fence earlier in the afternoon.

Any further progress round the course was out of the question now with the state that my clothes were in. Summoning up what little dignity I could in the circumstances, I thanked them and made the quickest way back across country to my car.

Julia was standing beside it. One glance at my general condition of muddy dishevelment and she opened the passenger-door.

'Get in,' she said, 'and don't you DARE to move from there, while I go and make our goodbyes.'

I did as I was bid, leant back against the head-rest, shut my eyes . . . and the world span gently away.

V

THE HUNT TERRIER-MEN

Sunday, 2 March to Monday, 10 March

I had made an exhibition of myself to an extent that she personally would take weeks to live down. Not only that but:–

  . . . I had sneaked out of the Masters' tent without having had the common decency to say goodbye and thank-you to my host and, although Rupert himself had been far too polite to say anything about it, he must have been offended.

  . . . by not telling Julia where I had been going, I had caused her to waste a large part of the afternoon looking for me.

  . . . she had had to drive me home, thereby missing the last two races.

  . . . she had been forced to forgo the 'evening of the point-to-point' party at Rupert's house, which she had enjoyed enormously last year and which I *knew* she had been looking forward to this year.

Furthermore, I had done the whole thing on purpose – and all because of this ridiculous obsession that I had recently acquired about Rupert. Oh yes, and when her stepmother, Dorothy, had rung me up at ten o'clock in the morning wanting to speak to me urgently, I had still been in no fit condition to be brought to the telephone and she had had to invent some story about my being out for the day. I was to go round and see her first thing when I got up to London on Monday morning.

The list of charges had taken most of the rest of Sunday at Thyrde House to enumerate and my request for a further offence to be taken into consideration before sentence was passed, that of failing to allow myself to be adequately killed during the Members' Race, had *not* been well received.

The part of all this that concerned me most had been the news that Dorothy had been trying to get in touch with me. I had by no means forgotten about her since we had last spoken on the telephone some three weeks before, but I had managed then to convince her that she had probably heard the last of the blackmail, and to ring her up and ask her if all was still well would only be to set her worrying again. None the less, I had been wondering constantly what, if any, Rupert's next move in her direction would be.

I was still wondering the next morning, all the way down the lorry-laden motorway to London. I would find out now, by the sound of it. I reached her flat at 10.30 a.m.

She seemed calm enough when she opened the door to me, outwardly – but it was hard to tell. She led me into the drawing-room without a word until we had both sat down. Then she spoke very quietly.

'He wants another ten thousand pounds. Said I'd broken my side of the bargain by talking about it. What can he mean, Derek? I only told you, and you're safe as houses?'

'Oh my God. . . . ' Suddenly I felt absolutely awful. It was my fault, nobody else's. By talking to Rupert Massingham as I had, I had only managed to precipitate the one thing that I had been trying to prevent. 'What are you going to do?' I said.

'Only one thing I can do. I can't raise the extra money. Or I could, I suppose, but he'd only come back asking for more. And more. No, I'm going to tell John now. I was going to as soon as I got the call early yesterday morning and then I remembered my promise to you.'

'Are you sure it's what you want?'

'Quite sure. It was the waiting that was far the worst thing. In a way it was a tremendous relief once I'd made up my mind.'

'Hold on, let me think for a minute,' I said.

When Dorothy had first told me about the blackmail, I had done my best to persuade her to tell her husband. Then later, once I had heard about the possibility of John Elton coming back into active politics, I had been equally vehement in trying to dissuade her. The first question, therefore, was would it be fair to Dorothy if I continued to do so?

Leaving that on one side for the moment, with what I now knew about Rupert, the prospect of his ever taking over from Charles Fortescue as Prime Minister was appalling. On present form, only Peter White, the Home Secretary, seemed to present a possible alternative, and whatever his latent qualities might prove to be – Jimmy McKay, for one, thought a lot of them – I myself doubted whether it was safe to rely on a lesser man than John Elton himself to beat Rupert to the top. Unless, of course, it should prove possible to show Rupert up for what he really was.

But if Rupert Massingham's true nature *were* to come out, on top of all the misfortunes that had been happening to other ministers over the past eighteen months, it could be enough to bring about the downfall of the whole government – unless there were someone else, again of the calibre of John, available to avert it. And with the story of his wife's complicity in her first husband's fraudulent deception over the jewellery brought out into the open, even he would at best fall short of the almost faultless image that made his return to politics such an attractive proposition and, at worst, he would present yet another embarrassment for the Government to overcome. And John, who would realise it at once, would never under those circumstances consider making a comeback at all.

Harking back to Dorothy, therefore, it had obviously not occurred to her yet that this would be the effect of telling her husband. But, even if John had not discussed his future plans with her, she must have read the speculation in the newspapers. How would she feel when she came to realise that it was entirely her fault his missing the chance of getting back into the one thing that he ever really wanted to do with his life?

There could be only one conclusion: John must not be told. Equally, Dorothy herself must be spared the agony and deprivation of trying to raise yet more money. I, who had brought about this second demand by my own meddling, owed her at least that.

'Look,' I said, 'I'll find the money this time. I've had a bit of a windfall lately.' It happened to be true. An aunt had died, leaving me a totally unexpected twenty thousand pounds, and I'd willingly spend half of it and more to stop Rupert – and incidentally buy even a small bit of extra time for John.

'Derek, you can't. I won't hear of it.' But the sunlight streaming through the windows lit up the sudden expression of eagerness that flashed on to her beautiful urchin face.

'No, wait. You yourself said that there wasn't any point in going on if it was only going to mean him coming back for more. What I'm suggesting is that we should use the money this time to try and trap the blackmailer. If we succeed, the courts are very good about that sort of thing, and you may not even have to tell John at all.

Certainly none of the story about your first husband and the diamonds need come out, and I'll stand a very good chance of getting my money back, too. Whereas, if we should fail and he does come back, you'll be able to tell John and you'll be no worse off then than you are now.'

She didn't reply for a full minute. Then:

'On one condition. Only if you let me pay you back if it fails. All of it.'

'We'll argue about that if and when the time comes. Now, tell me everything you can about that telephone call,' I said.

'Well, he started straight away by asking for the extra ten thousand. I protested it was unfair and that I'd kept my side of the bargain, and I've told you what his reply to that was. You haven't told anyone about me, have you?'

'No of course not,' I said, suffering as I did so severe pangs of conscience although the words themselves were strictly true. But I couldn't tell her about Rupert Massingham without letting on that I'd followed her that night and, although she hadn't actually told me not to, I felt that she might lose any confidence she might have in me if I did. 'You obviously didn't recognise his voice or you'd have said so, but was there anything about it that seemed in any way familiar?'

'Nun. .o. I don't think so. It was the same man as last time, I'm certain of that.'

'What else did he say?'

'I was to have a full eight days to find the money and I was to stay by the telephone from nine a.m., the Monday after next – that's today week – all day if necessary and I'd be given instructions as to how and where the money's to be handed over. And once again total secrecy, especially from the police.'

'Anything else?'

'It's to be put into a flat briefcase, one of those ones with a combination lock that you can buy at any of the big department stores. I'm to give him the combination when he rings. That's about all, I think.'

'What about the notes themselves? Any stipulations about those – small denominations, used, non-consecutive numbers and all that?'

'No, he didn't say anything about that but, then, he didn't last time, either.'

'Really?'

'Yes. A lot of them *were* used, of course; they mostly are nowadays. I had much more time to collect the money then, and I just got them together as and how I could, fives and tens mostly. They took up remarkably little space, too. I used a canvas holdall that time, and even for fifty thousand it only took really quite a small one to hold all that.'

'Right. Here's what we'll do,' I said.

I had decided on twenty-pound notes as being more easy to trace and identify than tens and fives, yet not likely to arouse so much suspicion as fifties. I had collected them from the bank on the Friday afternoon, five hundred of them in bundles of fifty each, secured round the middle by a red plastic band. 'There you go,' the young counter-clerk had said in the kindly manner of a corner-shop proprietor bestowing a bag of wine gums on a timid child. The whole consignment had been just over six inches by about three and a half, by two and a half inches thick.

I had decanted them into the briefcase early that morning, before leaving my house.

'Off for a day in the country?' Dorothy had said when I arrived at her flat promptly at 9 a.m. I had put on a tweed coat and cavalry-twill trousers rather than a suit as I hadn't been sure where I would have to go and what I would have to do. She seemed to be positively enjoying the whole thing, now. Even when the telephone rang for the first time, she walked over to it with a distinctly jaunty step.

'Hello.... Oh, it's you Yvonne.... No, we can't, I'm afraid.... Remind Sir John that we're dining with the Hiltons that night, will you? ... OK? Thank you.'

It was the first of three calls from John Elton's office in the City that day.

'Hello? ... Sally? ... Look, is it something important? ... Yes, I'm waiting for a really rather vital call.... Would you mind most awfully? ... Bless you. Goodbye.'

It was the first of five calls from assorted girlfriends of Dorothy's that day.

'Hello? ... Hello? ... Hello.'

She looked round at me and put her hand over the mouthpiece.

'There's no one there. I think he's hung up on me.'

It was the first of seven such calls whose only purpose could have been to alarm and dismay.

And they certainly had their effect. She was still relatively cheerful at one o'clock when we ate the lunch that she had cooked for us, but by 4.30 it was I who had to make the tea. At six o'clock I was in two minds as to whether to give her a drink to steady her, but I decided against it. I strongly suspected that once she'd started she'd need another, and she'd have some driving to do later. It was five minutes to nine, after nearly twelve hours of waiting, that the telephone rang for the sixteenth time.

'Hello.... Yes? ... Clapham Common, south side .... Hold on, I'll write that down.' She looked at me enquiringly, and I showed her the pen that I was holding at the ready. I doubted whether she herself could have written anything down legibly. She raised the receiver again and repeated the directions over to me, her voice lifeless and mechanical like that on an answering machine: 'Red Ford Fiesta ... in the boot, same as last time.... Registration number. . . . ' I wrote that down, too. 'Combination?' She looked at the telephone uncomprehendingly.

I held out the bit of paper on which I had written down the two numbers as I had set them that morning. No reaction. I waved it up and down in front of her. 'Briefcase,' I mouthed, and then she took it.

'Oh . . . yes . . . 586 left, 238 right.' She put the receiver down and turned back to me again.

'It's no good, Derek. I'm sorry, I just can't do it.'

'Oh, come on. . . .' And then I stopped. It was suddenly apparent that I couldn't possibly allow her to drive, the state that she was in. 'All right, I'll do it for you.'

'You . . . how . . .?'

'My trousers are much the same colour as yours, and I'll put on my Barbour. Just give me the keys of your car and lend me that headscarf of yours, and I'll bring them both back in the morning,' I said.

It was beginning to spot with rain when I found the three Terrier-men, Tom, Ted and Cully, waiting patiently where I had left them that morning, in my own car which was parked conveniently just behind Dorothy's.

'Slight change of plan,' I said. 'Lady Elton can't make it after all, and I'm going to take her place.'

I held out her headscarf to show them and, rather shamefacedly, demonstrated by holding it over my head. I had been afraid that they would laugh at me, but they went on listening attentively.

'One of you drive this car, if you will, and have a good look about you just in case we're being followed. Flash your lights once if you spot anyone and I'll try to lose him. I'll weave about the streets for a bit, in any case, and when you're sure that we're alone flash your lights three times. I'll acknowledge by turning off my rear lights once and then I'll make for the rendezvous. All clear so far?'

'Yes, Derek,' Tom said.

'Right. I'll have to drive off as soon as I've dumped the briefcase and I'll go straight home and wait for you there. Don't take any action whatever happenns and above all don't let him see you. Here's a rough map that I've drawn, showing where my house is in relation to the drop.'

Tom took it through open window and passed it to Cully in the front passenger-seat, who glanced at it, nodded once and put it in his pocket.

'Right, let's have the briefcase, then, and thank you all very much indeed.'

As I moved on to Dorothy's car, Ted, who always drove the Terrier-men's land-rover, got out from the back and took his seat at the wheel. I drove off through the backstreets, taking a right turn, then a left, then a left again and then another right before I saw Ted flash his lights three times. I acknowledged the signal and made straight for Vauxhall Bridge.

The plan that I had evolved was a relatively simple one, but I couldn't see how it could be bettered. Indeed, there didn't seem to be any way in which it could go wrong. I had a letter in my pocket from the bank manager, confirming that five hundred twenty-pound notes, numbers 28B 599001 to 599500 inclusive, had been issued to me on the previous Friday afternoon. I had shown this to the three Terrier-men that morning, and they had watched me put those actual notes into the briefcase and set the combination. The case had only just left their possession, and they would also see me put it into the boot of the Ford Fiesta.

I kept in the middle lane as I crossed the river, drove under the railway bridge and straight on. Once set on the road to Clapham, I glanced in the driving-mirror. The Terrier-men were still safely following behind in my own car.

The change in plan was only marginal and in fact made very little difference. I could no longer watch with Tom, Ted and Cully, as I would have done had we all been following Dorothy, but as I myself had actually seen Rupert Massingham collect the first batch of blackmail money my testimony would still be there to back up theirs. And they knew Rupert almost as well as I did and would be able to identify him positively as he took the briefcase from the place where I had put it or drove off in the actual car.

While I was negotiating the roundabout at Streatham, I had a moment of panic. It had started to rain quite heavily now and the reflection of lights on the wet tarmac made visibility difficult. There was a car behind me, but was it the right one? I slowed to a crawl, allowed it to overtake, and it wasn't them. Neither was the next one. But I should have had more faith in the terrier-men. The third car pulled in behind me, and I could see Ted's face grinning through the windscreen at me from behind the wheel.

I drove on until, leaving the little clock-tower by the Tube station on my right, I could see the strings of lamp-light criss-crossing through the bare trees of Clapham Common. I was within a hundred yards or so of the target now and I pulled in to the side of the road and adjusted the headscarf, hoping to goodness that I wouldn't be stopped by the police for any reason or, worse still, be seen by anyone I knew. My own car came by and drew up some sixty yards ahead of me. Cully got out. As I drove on past them again, he was wiping the windscreen with a yellow cloth.

The Ford Fiesta was exactly where Rupert had said it would be, parked in the little loop-road just short of the Old Windmill Inn. From my reflection in the glass of the side-window, I was pretty sure that I'd be able to get away with impersonating Dorothy if I didn't hang about. I double-checked the registration number from the bit of paper on which I had it written down, got out of the car and took the briefcase over, walking with the best that I could manage in the way of a feminine gait, opened the boot and put it in. Then I slammed the hatchback shut, walked back and drove off, pulling the headscarf down as I did so until it assumed the more respectable rôle of something round my neck. The whole operation had taken approximately thirty seconds – just long enough, I hoped, for the watching Terrier-men to be able to vouch for my action but still not quite long enough for Rupert to realise who I was.

Dorothy had arranged for John to take Julia down to the country that evening, to dine with an unmarried sister of his and stay the night afterwards. He was to have picked her up, on his way from the City, at the shop where she now worked and deliver her back there the following morning, thereby avoiding the possibility of either of them getting any idea as to what might be going on. At the same time, it would leave Dorothy's flat and my house free for whatever eventuality might arise.

I let myself in through the front door, went into the drawing-room and sat down and waited. As soon as the Terrier-men came and joined me, I would ring up a police superintendent friend of mine and tell him the whole story. I had already found out that he would be at home that evening and I had warned him that I might be telephoning, although not yet what about. With any luck, and if everyone got a move on, Rupert would be caught with the briefcase still on him. But, if that should fail, there was every possibility of catching him spending at least some of the twenty-pound notes or disposing of them in some other way. I had been surprised to learn that he had not made any stipulation about the notes being used and with numbers not easy to identify. It hadn't done him any harm last time because Dorothy had insisted on paying up without taking any steps to warn the police. Perhaps he had become over-confident and, if that were so, this might just be the one mistake that Rupert Massingham had yet made.

I looked at my watch. How long had Rupert taken to appear out of the shadows and drive the van off last time – five minutes . . . ten? Then there was the drive back here from the other side of the Common – say, another ten. No need to worry yet, I supposed.

Once I had set things in motion, I planned to ring up Tom Lavenham and warn him what was likely to happen. Then I would have the irrefutable proof that would satisfy even Julia that I had a case against Rupert. And, if we chose the right opportunity, it might even be possible to tell John Elton about it in such a way as would not prejudice the decision that he must soon be going to make.

Still no sign of Tom, Ted and Cully. And then another thought struck me. I myself had driven exactly the same distance that they would have to and, allowing for the fact that I knew the area and they didn't, the time that it took them to arrive after me shouldn't be much more than the time they had had to watch until Rupert arrived and drove off in the Ford Fiesta.

It was then that I really started to worry. What on earth could have happened to them? Could Rupert be planning to leave the car until morning and not pick it up that night at all? Hardly likely with all that money in it. Had the Terrier-men been picked up by the police for loitering? Had the rough map that I had drawn not been good enough? I wished to God now that I'd thought of writing my telephone number, which was ex-directory, on the top of it. Could anything worse have happened? Should I go back and look for them? But, if I did that, what if they came while I was away?

These were the thoughts that went jumbling through my mind as I waited. And went on waiting. It was gone three o'clock in the morning when I heard the knocking on the door.

I ran and opened it and there, in the glow from the outside light and on his own, stood Cully holding his cap awkwardly out in front of him with both his hands.

'Thank God you're here,' I said to him. 'But where are Tom and Ted?'

'I'm took 'em to the horspital. You'd best come quick, Derek, you'll be too late else. I think Ted are dying,' he said.

VI

LOOSE HORSE

Tuesday, 11 March to Monday, 17 March

I couldn't remember hearing Cully himself ever actually say anything before – certainly I had never seen him without the other two. He spoke softly, with a slightly husky voice and total economy of words. He led me out to my car and assumed the driving-seat as though it were a matter of course, while I equally automatically got in on the passenger side. He told me everything that had happened, along the way.

'We watches from behind, like you says, and Sir Rupert he never turn up, see? Then these four young tearaways comes out from the bushes and starts monkeying about with the boot of the Ford car. Well, I know you says not to get involved like, but we wasn't going to let 'em take your money, Derek, was we? I keeps two of 'em busy, learnt to take care of meself in the Navy, end of the war, see; but the others takes a knife and one of them brass-knuckle things to Tom and Ted, and when I'm got a moment to look to them they all four gets into the car and makes theirselves scarce. It were then that I seen Sir Rupert weren't coming – he be sent them instead.'

'Oh my God, I *am* sorry.' The whole scheme had seemed so foolproof at the time, but I ought to have realised that if anything had gone wrong the Terrier-men were not the sort of people to stand by and do nothing. How could I have been so stupid as not to have foreseen at least the possibility of something like this happening and thus to put at risk such old and loyal friends? 'What did you do then?' I said.

'Ted were unconscious, see, but I gets him and Tom into the back seat and drives 'em orf to the horspital. St Thomas' they calls it. They operates on Ted right away.'

'What are his chances?'

Cully shook his head. 'I don't know, Derek. Lucky it weren't Tom, though – it's his heart, see. Carries his little bottle of tablets around regular, does Tom.'

'How *is* Tom?'

'We won't be entering Tom for no beauty contest yet awhile. Broke his hand, they done, and cut his face up proper.' He cast his eyes towards the roof of the car. 'Blood!'

My involuntary glance over my shoulder to the back seat was, to my shame, intercepted by Cully.

'Don't you fret about that, Derek. I'm sponged it down for you,' he said.

Cully drove with the same care and expertise that characterised everything he did. He never went above the speed-limit of 30 miles per hour, but the traffic seemed to open up in front of him to let him through and the lights changed to green as he came to them.

'Have you told the police?'

'The horspital done that. Reckoned you'd want to be kept out of it, Derek. Told 'em you'd lent us your car for the day and we got lorst driving it back to your house for you when we happened on them four acting suspicious-like and tried to stop 'em.' Again the eyes cast roofwards, scornful this time. 'Lorst, me!'

And I saw at once that the suggestion was as preposterous in the streets of London as it would have been among the green lanes and cart-tracks of the Northamptonshire countryside.

The doctor – he was the registrar as I was to learn later – was coming out through the double swing-doors as Cully and I approached the intensive treatment unit. He was earnest, bespectacled and reassuring, with a white coat, and a stethoscope worn round his neck in a position of constant readiness. He came forward to meet us.

'Ah, Cully,' he said.

'This is Lord Thyrde I were telling you of. How is he, Doctor?'

'Mr Edward Bannister? Holding his own, thanks to you largely.' He turned to me, 'If our friend here hadn't acted so promptly, I doubt if we'd have had a chance of saving him at all.'

'Can you tell me about his injuries?' I said.

'They're extensive, I'm afraid. Let's see now: fractured parietal – that's a plate of bone above the ear – a small fracture of the mandible' – he put a hand to his own jawbone – 'fractured nose, collapsed lung, ruptured spleen and blood in the urine. He's had surgery for the spleen and a chest-drain, and we've had to give him a tracheostomy to help him breathe. Oh yes, and he's broken his leg badly. We've got it on traction for the moment, but . . . we'll have to operate later.'

His tone implied a certain amount of doubt as to whether such a necessity would in fact ever arise.

I asked him the same question that I had asked Cully. 'What do you think his chances are?'

The doctor shook his head slowly. 'Fifty–fifty. Less than that, perhaps.'

'Can I see him?' I said.

'I think you should, if only for his brother's sake. Mr Thomas Bannister's been asking for you repeatedly, and I doubt if he'll settle till he's seen you. His injuries were only superficial, but we took an electrocardiogram – routine because of his angina – and I'm afraid it showed up a small myo-cardial infarction, so to be on the safe side we've put him in the ITU as well.'

'Myo-cardial . . . ?'

'Damage to the wall of the heart. We're keeping an eye on that and we've got a nurse permanently with the pair of them. Sister's expecting you. Only five minutes, mind. Cully'll take you in.'

I had been struck by the fact that here, just as everywhere else he went, Cully had immediately become known as 'Cully' and commanded instinctive liking and respect.

I had never been in an intensive treatment unit before. The room was an E-shape but without the middle bar, and the beds which faced outwards from the walls were interspersed with what I believe are known as 'units' and carry all the impedimenta necessary for treatment. My immediate impression was one of intense silence, but I became aware of an underlying sound, a sort of muted but regular blipping coming from the electronic equipment. The nearest I can get to it is that of the slow regular drip of a tap on to water, from no great height but some way away. Cully introduced me to the Sister, whose desk was by the door.

As far as I could see, only the two beds were occupied at the moment. These were served by the units on the outer side of each, a uniformed nurse busying herself noiselessly but efficiently with various pieces of equipment on the left-hand one. The one in the middle had been removed – presumably so that the two brothers could see each other – but at the moment both had their eyes shut. Ted, I knew, was unconscious, and Tom must have dropped off at last.

Cully immediately went and took up a position standing between the two beds, with his back to the wall, so that the three of them once again assumed the formation in which I had always seen them. Tom on the right propped up with pillows, one arm in a sling with the little finger of that hand splinted, the skin of his face pale with a slightly translucent quality to it against which the line of neat black stitching that traversed his fleshless cheek stood out prominently, a distinct tinge of blue around his lips. Ted on the left, propped up, too, stitches on his forehead, a pair of black eyes – they were the least of his problems – tubes everywhere, one from his nose leading to a bottle with a kind of greenish substance in it, one from the base of his throat to a ventilator, two from drips into his right arm – blood and some sort of clear liquid, respectively – a tube from his chest leading to God knows where and another from beneath his white hospital gown to what I strongly suspected of being a urine-bag attached to the bed. Cully in the middle motionless, an expression of paternal solicitude on his kindly weatherbeaten face.

Tom stirred and opened his eyes, then, as he focused on me, he tried to sit up.

'For goodness' sake, don't move,' I said. I found myself echoing Cully's gladness that it hadn't been Tom with his bad heart who had been so badly injured. Although the two brothers were so similar – why, I couldn't say, perhaps he was marginally the more forceful character – I had somehow always had a sneaking preference for Tom.

'We'm . . . we'm let you down. I'm sorry, Derek,' he said as he subsided again.

'Of course you haven't, Tom. I'm the one who's here to apologise.' The contrition in his voice had made my feeling of guilt at what I had allowed to happen to the two brothers even greater. 'Thank you for what you all did. It was far more than I had any right to expect.'

He shook his head firmly. 'No, we'm promised to help, Derek, and we'm not, see?'

It was Cully, not the sister, who beckoned me firmly outside well within the stipulated five-minute maximum.

'Look,' I said, 'I'll stay here for a bit. You go off and get some rest and I'll call you if you're needed.'

'*No*,' the tone of Cully's voice showed that any further argument would be pointless, 'thanking you, all the same, Derek. I'll be staying here. Since the wife died, Tom and Ted they're all I'm got, see?'

I shook his hand and left him, a sure bastion at the door of his stricken friends.

I returned Dorothy's car and headscarf to her in the morning.

'Did your plan work?' she asked.

'No, I'm afraid not,' I said. Somehow I hadn't told her that the Terrier-men were to be my witnesses and I was only too glad of it now. She'd have been bound to hear about what had happened to Tom and Ted, and that would have been on her conscience, too. Not only was I determined, out of fairness to her, that it should remain where it properly belonged – on mine – but also I was pretty certain that it would mean my being totally unable to prevent her from immediately confessing everything to John.

'I'm so sorry,' she said, but I detected a distinct tone of relief in her voice and, luckily, she didn't pursue the subject further. 'Oh, Derek, will it stop now?'

Actually, this was another thing that had been worrying me. Rupert was bound to be told what had happened by his minions, and I was pretty sure that he would regard this as another breach of his instructions to Dorothy and might well feel entitled to demand yet more as a result of it. But there was no point in worrying Dorothy unnecessarily, so

I gave what I suppose comes into the category of what is derisively referred to as a 'politician's answer'.

'I hope so,' I said.

Julia was upstairs in the bedroom when I got back from the House of Lords that evening. She didn't look up from the dressing-table as I came through the door and, when I walked over and put a hand on each of her shoulders, she went on applying blue make-up to her eyes as though I hardly existed.

'Hello,' I said.

No reply, not even a pause in the operation. I glanced round at the pictures on the walls, late-Victorian water-colours of the village of Thyrde. There was a horse-drawn baker's van standing outside a cottage door in one of them, otherwise they differed very little in appearance from the way the village looks today.

'How was dinner with Aunt Mildred?'

'Bloody!' she said.

'Oh dear, I'm so sorry. What happened?'

'She and my father spent half the evening asking me when you and I were going to get married and the other half reading me a lecture on getting myself talked about with Rupert.' She turned and glared at me. 'Did you put Daddy up to it?'

'No, I swear I didn't.'

'Oh.' There seemed to be a marginal softening of the atmosphere, but I still doubted whether it was going to turn out to be one of the jolliest of evenings. 'Look, Derek, there really *is* nothing in it. Why don't we invite Rupert to dinner here and then everyone will see there isn't?'

I stared at her. After what he had caused to happen to the Terrier-men even the suggestion of sitting down at the same table as Rupert appalled me. But Julia had gone back to her make-up and was oblivious of the consternation that must have shown in my face.

'We really do owe him for an awful lot of hospitality already. And there's that enormous party of his next Monday that we're going to. You haven't forgotten about that, I suppose?'

I had – totally. It was the London counterpart of Rupert's 'evening of the point-to-point' party at his house in Northamptonshire and Julia and I had been among the few people who had been included in both invitation-lists. I had agreed, reluctantly even then, to Julia accepting for us and it didn't make me feel any better to be reminded of it now.

'I'm sorry, darling, I don't want us to go,' I said.

Julia slammed the little pot of blue gunge down on the glass top of the dressing-table top and glared round at me.

'May I remind you, you wrecked the point-to-point for me and you made me miss the party afterwards by the disgusting state you got yourself into? Do you really expect me to give this one up, too?'

What little patience I had been managing to preserve instantly evaporated.

'Look, I've told you before that I do happen to know for a fact that Rupert Massingham is a very nasty bit of work indeed and I've also explained to you that I can't tell you why. Can't you get that into your thick head? We're not going – and that's final.'

'Is that so?' Julia smiled with her mouth, but those grey-green eyes had assumed an intensity that was lethal. 'That's up to you of course; it takes two to make a "we". *I'm* going,' she said.

In the end we both went. There had been an uneasy truce between us in the days that intervened, and Julia had been subdued but quite pleasant as we were changing for the party. It was only when I was negotiating Hyde Park Corner *en route* for the Transatlantic, the massive new hotel that had only just opened off the Bayswater Road, that she first spoke on the way.

'Will you promise me something, Derek?'

'Yes,' I said rashly.

'I've been trying to understand your point of view, I really have, but if you insist on coming in to the party, in spite of what you think about Rupert, do at least be polite to him.'

'I promise.'

'No, I know you. I don't mean just ignore him. Talk to him. Be nice to him if you possibly can. After all, he is our host.'

'I'll try,' I said.

I dropped her off at the ballroom entrance and drove off round the back until I was lucky enough to find an entirely deserted little side-street consisting of blocks of unlit offices. I parked the car and locked it. As I walked back to the front of the hotel again, I can't say that I was exactly relishing the prospect of the evening that lay ahead.

The room in which the party was held was enormous, chandeliers weeping down from the white and gold ceiling in a manner more reminiscent of an October-evening seafront than the Edwardian drawing-room that it was intended to represent. There were pillars everywhere, and from tables surrounding the foot of each of them white-hatted chefs dispensed from piled sides of smoked salmon and plates loaded with shellfish. With admirable staffwork, Rupert Massingham had contrived to arrange a day that was light of business in both Houses of Parliament, a lot of the faces that I was able to pick out I recognised to a greater or lesser extent and, from the crowded state of the room, most of the guests must already have arrived.

Our host himself was still standing near the door to receive stragglers, and Julia, the most recent arrival, was chattering away excitedly to him. With them stood the very pretty redhead whom I recognised at once from some sixteen days before as having been among the crowd in the Masters' tent at the point-to-point. My instant feeling of revulsion on seeing Rupert was replaced by a detached and almost clinical interest in how someone whose recent treatment of both Dorothy and the Terrier-men had been so iniquitous could preside as calmly and with such outward charm over a gathering like this.

There was nothing I could do about him now, however, and it was getting more and more doubtful as to whether there would be in the future. Anyway, I myself was on my best behaviour – for tonight at any rate. I helped myself to a glass of whisky and water from the tray of a passing waiter and went over to join them.

'Sorry we were late, Rupert.'

'Ah, Derek. This is Derek Thyrde,' he said to the girl beside him. 'Derek's a very important person.' His voice took on a tone of mock awe. 'He's a Whip in the Lords, no less – the House that *really* matters.' He turned back to me again. 'Isn't that right, dear? Do you know Camberley Roberts? Look after her, will you, while I take this charming girl of yours round for a bit?'

'Yes, of course. . . .' But Rupert had already whisked Julia off into the throng, leaving me uncertain as to whether I was more put out by this typical behaviour on his part or by my failure so far to carry out my undertaking to her.

I looked at my new charge doubtfully, because I couldn't be sure just how much she might be tied in with Rupert. Camberley Roberts had a delightfully moulded pink and white face; wide luminous eyes that I couldn't quite make

109

up my mind as to whether they were dark blue or violet; a definitely sensuous mouth and a figure to dream about; but by far her most distinctive feature was her hair, of a gloriously silky texture and the exact colour of a fox's – not quite long enough, perhaps, to enable her to play Lady Godiva in a church pageant with impunity, but well below shoulder-length. I could certainly have done a good deal worse in the way of a consolation prize.

'Didn't I see you from a distance at the Yardley point-to-point?' I said.

'Yes, but we met before that.'

I looked her slowly up and down. Then I shook my head.

'It just isn't possible. I couldn't have forgotten.'

'Out hunting, the Long Mile Goss day. Rupert's acting unpaid whipper-in, remember?'

She had a slightly twisted grin that left one very white tooth superimposed on her lower lip in a way that I some-how found incredibly attractive.

I looked again.

'Good God. You were the girl in the blue and white hunt collar, but most of that hair of yours was hidden under your cap, so it's not fair. Even so, how could I have failed to recognise you?'

The eyes glinted. Violet definitely, I decided.

'What rotten luck,' I said, 'your missing the end of the hunt like that.'

'Oh, I don't know. I was there for most of it – which was more than everyone else was. But, I say, are you actually a Whip in the Lords, or was that just Rupert teasing? Tell me about it,' she said.

'Well, it's an odd sort of job, but— ' And then I was interrupted.

The voice came from behind me. 'Derek? I'm so sorry, but could you spare a moment?' It was Dorothy Elton. Tentative. Apologetic. Oh my God, I thought, not again!

'Yes, of course. Will you forgive me, Camberley? Don't go away. I'll come back and find you,' I said.

'Derek, you'll never guess what's happened.' We had withdrawn to the comparative privacy of the side of the room. 'I've got them back.'

'*What*! Not the papers?'

'Yes.' Dorothy could hardly stand still for excitement. 'The document relating to the loan itself; valuation; photograph of the jewellery; the lot.'

'But . . . how did it happen?'

'Well, every Monday morning I leave the dirty sheets, pillow-cases and things in a box outside the door of the flat for the laundryman to collect, and he brings back last week's at the same time. I was out for most of the day and when I got back this evening I remember noticing that the strap was undone and, when I got the box inside and opened it up, there they were . . . just lying on the top.'

'I *am* glad,' I said, and it was indeed a tremendous weight off my mind to feel that my further meddling hadn't done yet more harm.

'Oh, Derek, you can't imagine the bliss of it, just knowing that I haven't got to tell John and that I'll never have to worry about it again. You'll forget I ever told you anything, too? Promise?' I nodded feebly, and Dorothy grabbed forward with both hands and kissed me. 'Bless you for all you've done. Now, go back to your gorgeous redhead,' she said.

It was no bad idea, but as I retraced my steps half of my mind was on more serious matters. Dorothy's appeal had effectively closed any chance I might have had of connecting Rupert with the blackmail. Still, with her completely and, with any luck, permanently restored to her old self again, John Elton might well feel that he could accept the candidature of Gloucestershire East and from there to getting into the Cabinet might be a relatively short step. His presence there now would be even more essential than before.

When I got back to the place where I had been talking to her, Camberley wasn't there.

I was buttonholed instead by a junior minister from the Commons who launched into an interminable story, and then by another from the Lords who wanted advice on various procedural matters of total unimportance, both of them oblivious to the impatience that must have been only too obvious from the expression on my face.

Remembering the undertaking that I had given before the party started, I was now beginning to have a bit of a conscience about Rupert and I thought that, before anything else, I'd better find him. I soon caught sight of him in the distance, but he was still with Julia and that presented me with a quandary. If I went up to them now, I knew from bitter experience that I might be accused of not trusting her. If I didn't, I would be ignoring him. The only really safe thing to do was to go back to looking for Camberley because, after all, it was Rupert himself who had put me in charge of her and, if I was with her, I couldn't be said to be slighting him.

'Derek!' I turned to find my boss, Patrick Oldfield, who had been standing talking to a group of people two or three yards away from me. In his hand was a two-thirds-full glass of what looked like pure orange juice, which I knew he would be making last the whole party, even though I knew that orange juice was what it would solely be. 'I'm surprised to see *you* here,' he said.

'Rupert Massingham's a neighbour of mine in the country.'

'Oh, I see.' And he turned back to his group again. It sounded no more than a polite cocktail-party answer, but I knew that this piece of intelligence would be docketed carefully away in his memory, to be called up again if ever he should have further cause to consider Rupert in relation to me.

I resumed my search in earnest, and after a bit I began to panic. I couldn't find either Rupert or Camberley – nor even Julia to whom I could at least explain my predicament.

'Hello, Derek.' This time it was the wife of another minister, a rather bossy lady at whom I had made a desultory pass during another, though less lavish, political party some weeks back, only to find it reciprocated with a good deal more enthusiasm than I had expected or indeed wanted.

'Hello, Peggy.'

'Charlie's not here tonight,' she said. 'He's had to go up to the constituency.'

'Julia iss.' I tried to sound more disappointed than I actually felt. She was moderately attractive, though not in the same class as Camberley.

'Oh.' Then she assumed a conspiratorial expression and spoke quietly through her teeth, without her lips moving. 'Watch out, she's coming up behind you. She doesn't suspect anything, does she . . . about *us*?'

There hadn't been anything to suspect, but I let that pass.

'No, why?'

'She looks pretty furious about something,' Peggy said.

Julia did indeed arrive blazing, and it only took one look from her for the hapless Peggy to shrink away into the throng. I cast an envious glance after her, wishing that such a retreat was open to me.

'Hello, darling,' I said.

'Don't "darling" me. How dare you, Derek, ostentatiously ignoring poor Rupert, like that.'

'Yes, but— '

' "But" nothing! I didn't want you to come and I knew exactly how you'd behave if you did. You've been stumping around all evening with a face like thunder. If that's what you think of your promises to me, I'm not going to put up with it any longer. Why should I? I'm leaving,' she said.

To hell with it, I thought, as she blazed off again. So much for my good intentions and genuine efforts – not to mention, once again, *her* stepmother. Never mind, she'd come round. She always did. No point in breaking my back over Rupert now, though, so I went on looking for Camberley instead.

But I still couldn't find her.

I found Peter White, the Home Secretary, looking distraught for some reason and very different from the capable personality that I had watched performing at the Home Affairs Committee. He nodded vaguely to me, but I couldn't help his problems. I had enough of my own.

I found Jimmy McKay, holding a full glass of dark brown liquid. He waved happily to me with the bottle in his other hand, the label of which I didn't have any difficulty in recognising.

I found innumerable other people, none of whom I wanted to see.

Then there was a loud banging sound, and a hundred conversations stopped abruptly.

Rupert Massingham was standing in the doorway, Julia beside him with one of her hands threaded loosely through his arm.

'Sorry to interrupt, but we've got to go now. Plenty to eat and drink – it's all paid for. Stay as long as you like,' he said.

And they went.

Suddenly I became aware, standing only a couple of yards away from me, of the elusive Camberley and at the same moment she noticed me. We stared at each other in silence, frozen on her face an expression of outraged disbelief that I knew would find its exact counterpart on my own. Then her features relaxed into that twisted grin again.

'Snap!' she said.

I asked her to come and have dinner with me, and she said "yes". They were hardly auspicious circumstances but, such as they were, they were common to both of us. And there wasn't much else for either of us to do.

'Hold on here and I'll bring the car round.'

'No, it can't be far. I'll come with you. Give me a moment to go and get my coat,' she said.

My car was still the only one in the dismal backstreet where I had left it. Four youths in jeans and black leather coats were jostling each other down the pavement towards us. I got out the key and started to open the passenger-door.

'Are you Viscount *turd*?' said the foremost one, a particularly unprepossessing specimen with the tumescence of past and present acne adorning his rat-like face and two thin little gold rings, one above the other, in holes pierced in his left ear. The other three sniggered at the brilliant wit of their leader. But it was an insult to which I myself had become quickly immune during my earliest days as a lower boy at Eton – though, oddly enough, never at my private school, an establishment not noted for its reticence in scatological terminology.

'What of it?' I said.

'We was to give you a message. I got it 'ere.'

He put his right hand into his pocket and drew out something that glinted. Even in that dim light I was able to recognise the five connected brass rings of a knuckleduster as he began to tap it ominously against the palm of his left. I pulled the passenger-door open and thrust the car-key at Camberley.

'Drive off, quick as you can,' I hissed. 'Get the police. I can cope with this.'

115

Then, with my hand held out as though to receive the nonexistent written message, I walked slowly forward until I was within reach of him and hit him, as hard as I could, on his nasty face.

He staggered backwards. 'We'll do 'im, Ralph,' said one of the others from behind me. The 'l' in his name was pronounced apparently. But Ralph was by no means as immobilised as I had hoped.

'You fucking keep out of this,' he said, 'this fucker's mine,' and he lurched forward again, swiping simultaneously with the as yet hand-held knuckleduster to inflict a glancing but none the less painful blow on my cheek and jaw.

I had had the advantage of surprise but I knew that it wouldn't last and that my schoolboy boxing was no match for the more sophisticated elements of street-fighting. I managed to hit him again, less hard this time and solely because defence seemed to form only a minor part of Ralph's strategy. I could hear sounds of movement behind me from the other three, but obediently they showed no signs of joining in. I had no illusions, though, that in the unlikely event of my coming out on top the embargo imposed on them would be deemed to be no longer relevant. My only hope, and it was a slim one, was to keep things going long enough for help to arrive.

I took another wild swing at him, he side-stepped and I nearly fell, recovering myself but just not quickly enough. It still gave Ralph the respite he needed to slip the knuckleduster on to the fingers of his right hand. For what seemed like seconds, but it could only have been a fraction of that, I saw his lips parting in a grin of satisfaction as he drew his hand back, and it was with a sense of resigned inevitability that I awaited the appalling prospect of the impact to come.

Then, totally unexpectedly, he froze solid. I could see him staring over and beyond my shoulder, his jaw dropped and a look of almost comical bewilderment came over his face. 'Cor, fuck!' he said and bolted.

I swivelled round, so astonished at this phenomenon that my eagerness to find out what could possibly have caused it even put feelings of relief into second place.

There was the car, passenger-door still open. There, prone on the pavement between us, arranged in a neat pattern like cod in the window-display of an old-fashioned fishmonger's, lay his three inert comrades. Whilst, leaning against the railings, the indulgent expression with which she had been watching my efforts still on her face, stood Camberley Roberts, the car-key with its red garage-tag swinging gently backwards and forwards from the finger of one gloved hand.

The tooth materialised.

'I *am* the police,' she said.

VII

THE GIRL IN THE DISTINCTIVE HUNT COLLAR

Monday, 17 March to Tuesday, 18 March

'But how on earth did you do it?' I said, looking across the table at her in the dim light of the restaurant. 'Three of them at once! It was only sheer luck that stopped me being murdered by my poor *one*.'

'It all happened rather quickly really but give me a moment or two and I'll see if I can reconstruct it for you.' Camberley put down the menu, in which she had been engrossed, with a certain amount of reluctance. Neither of us had had a chance to get anything to eat at the party.

'Right. You remember when your chap asked the other three in such delicate terms not to intervene?'

'Yes.'

'Well, two of them decided to stop me getting away. I wasn't going to, actually, but they stood on either side of me holding a wrist and an elbow each, and the third one noticed the bag that I had on my shoulder, took out a knife and came forward with his other hand reaching for the strap, presumably with the intention of cutting it. You'd have thought he could have at least *asked* me to take it off first, but I suppose he thought it would be more fun that way. Cost quite a bit, that bag did, and I'm rather fond of it, so I kicked him none too gently in the groin and he fell down clutching himself. I expect you were rather too busy to notice the noises he was making at the time.'

'And that was him out of the way?'

'Only temporarily, I'm afraid. The other two seemed slightly shaken. I don't think they'd been expecting anything quite like that, and the great thing of course is always to keep the initiative. So I pulled against the chap on my right, got him off balance so that he had to put a foot forward between mine, and lunged back towards him, tripping him and elbowing him in the throat as he fell.'

She was leaning forward, a distant smile on that beautifully moulded pink and white face of hers, totally absorbed in what she was saying and describing all this as though it were a rally in a game of tennis.

'What then?'

'Well, the man on the left wasn't going to allow anything like that to happen to *him*. He let go with his right hand so that he could put his arm round my throat – all this was taking a matter of seconds, mind you – but I managed to wrench my left wrist free, got both sets of fingers between his elbow and my neck and leant forward pulling him over my right shoulder and on to the ground – where I'm sorry to say he hit his head on the kerb. That one really was out of the fight, but the man who had been on my right had managed to get up again and came up and grabbed the lapels of my coat. I put my left elbow on top of his forearm, gripped my own wrist with the fingers of my right hand and levered him down into a kneeling position where I brought my knee, this time, sharply up into the lower part of his chin. That only left the knife man, who had taken rather longer to recover. I must have hurt him quite a lot, because he was in such a blind rage that he came at me with the knife in earnest, meaning to plunge it into my midriff, which is the easiest to deal with of all.'

119

She paused and looked up at me. Her hair had this quality of the finest silk about it as it glinted red in the candle-light.

'And that's really all there was to it.'

'You might have lent a hand with my one,' I said ruefully. 'I damn nearly got the full benefit of that knuckleduster of his.'

Camberley's violet eyes were innocent.

'But . . . I thought you were enjoying it,' she said.

There was a pause.

'Seriously, though, I could give you a spot of coaching in that sort of thing, if you'd like me to.'

'I would indeed.'

She nodded. 'Mightn't be a bad idea, either – if we're to work together,' she said.

Very much to my surprise, Camberley had insisted on leaving the three youths where they lay on the pavement. My own inclination would have been to try to find out all that we could from them first, but now that she had told me who she was I couldn't very well argue. I also rather cravenly felt that the sooner we got away from that particular area the better, just in case the leader should recover his nerve enough to come back with that knuckleduster of his and carry on where he had left off. I had driven her to the restaurant where we were now sitting, a favourite of mine but one which I hadn't been to lately because Julia seemed to have taken against it. The head waiter had welcomed me as a long-lost friend and Camberley as an adornment to any establishment. He had given us my usual table by the wall.

'Work together?' I said.

'Come now, that was no ordinary mugging. He knew your name, somebody must have told him. Rupert?'

I stared at her. 'So you're on to him, too, but— '

120

'Not here. Can we meet tomorrow morning some-where?'

'I've got a room at the House of Lords. We wouldn't be disturbed there.'

'That sounds fine. Nine-thirty? Come on now, tell me about your job as a whip,' she said.

I explained to her about what being a Lord-in-Waiting meant in political terms, that I was acting as Deputy Chief Whip in my immediate superior's enforced absence, what that job entailed and how, with any luck, I hoped to get the appointment permanently – provided that I hadn't totally damned myself in Patrick Oldfield's eyes, that is. She seemed to be genuinely interested.

Then we talked about the hunt from Long Mile Goss. A farmer's daughter from a remote but highly sought after hunting-country somewhere up in the north, Rupert had put her on point duty outside the covert and she had had to stay behind for long enough to make sure that all twenty-six-and-a-half couple were on before catching us up. Even so, she had managed to see the best of the day.

Altogether I hadn't enjoyed an evening so much for weeks. I realise now that it was probably the combi-nation of reaction from the fight itself and relief at what had seemed at the time to be certain disaster having ended so satisfactorily that drove all accumulated wor-ries, at least temporarily, out of my mind. The state of euphoria that I was in lasted right up to the time that I dropped Camberley back at her flat in Wandsworth. Even then, it was only tarnished slightly by a sudden pang of totally unreasoning jealousy. I knew that Rupert actually lived on the other side of the river, somewhere within the division-bell area in Pimlico. Could it have been from here that he had been returning, on those mornings when I became aware of the silver BMW, DWK 49 T?

121

But, the moment I started on the short drive back home to Clapham, the full horror of the situation came flooding back to me, all the problems and uncertainty of the past weeks with Julia, culminating in that scene in the doorway of the Transatlantic Hotel ballroom. I glanced at my watch, it was long after midnight, and I braced myself for the awful row that was bound to happen as soon as I got back. Then another thought struck me, that she might not be there at all, and I couldn't make up my mind as to which would be worse. When she had said she was going to leave me, did she mean just for that evening or was it to be for good? I turned my key in the door.

The house was empty, and I was half-relieved, half-worried. I waited up for a full forty minutes, but there was still no sign of her. Then I went miserably to bed and, eventually, to sleep.

'Right,' said Camberley, 'I mustn't ask you to break any confidences of course, but first of all tell me anything you can about how your political colleagues view Rupert Massingham.'

She had arrived punctually at nine-thirty. I was sitting at the desk in my office, she on a chair the other side of it, but it was clear from the beginning that it was Camberley who was very much in charge. After my somewhat abortive single-handed campaign, I found this to be a tremendous relief.

'They think he's wonderful.'

She looked up sharply. 'Haven't they got any suspicions about him, then?'

'I don't think so.' I remembered my interview with Patrick Oldfield. 'No, I'm sure not. Everything I know about him I've found out for myself.'

'I see. And that is?'

'Principally that he's involved in blackmail.'

This time there was a noticeable pause.

Then, 'Blackmail? Tell me about it,' Camberley said.

'Well, I can't give you the name concerned, because I promised not to – especially to the police. And I can't even tell you what the blackmail was about, because that might be a giveaway, too. But apart from that. . . .' And I told her how I had come to be involved, starting with my noticing the BMW ahead of me while I was stuck in that traffic jam in the Wandsworth Road.

When I described how I had seen it disappearing into what I had a distinct impression of being a tunnel – the part that the tunnel itself had played in the story had completely slipped my own memory over the past few weeks – Camberley looked up from the pad on which she had been taking notes.

'How strong was the impression?'

'Pretty strong, but I went back and looked the next day and couldn't find any sign of it at all.'

'Right, we can come back to the tunnel later. Go on, Derek.'

I told her about the visit to the friend's flat, the eventual admission to being blackmailed, how I had followed the friend's car surreptitiously and witnessed the depositing of the first lot of blackmail money, followed by my identification of Rupert under the lamp-light.

Then I went on to tell her everything that had happened since, my lunch with Jimmy McKay, the confrontation with Rupert, what he had done to me at the point-to-point, the second blackmail demand and the part played by the Terrier-men and, finally, the return of the papers themselves, although I didn't say that I had only been told about this at the party the night before.

'So what have you actually got to connect Rupert with this blackmail of yours?' Camberley asked when I had finished. 'One glimpse of his face under a street-lamp caught

123

from a distance and the van with the odd name which led to your finding out about the blackmail in the first place? Did you get the registration number of the Glocksfoot van?'

'No, there wasn't any reason to when it was in the yard and, to tell you the truth, I didn't think of it in Regent's Park that night. There wouldn't have been a lot of point to it once I'd seen Rupert himself,' I added defensively.

'So there's no way of knowing it was the same van; there could be several, and coincidences do happen.'

'There's no "Glocksfoot" in the telephone book,' I said.

'That doesn't mean anything; it might be a subdivision of a larger company. Just how certain are you that it was him under the lamp?'

'Ninety-nine per cent.'

'But could you go into the witness-box and swear to it – under oath?'

I was beginning to feel more like the prisoner in the dock. 'I suppose not. But there's always the BMW – we might be able to trace that DWK number to him.'

'No need to. I happen to know it's his, but that only connects him with the tunnel, not with the blackmail. Perhaps you had subconsciously recognised Rupert as the driver that morning, so your mind was preconditioned to being misled by a chance resemblance to him of the man in Regent's Park. He never actually admitted anything when you confronted him, did he?'

'No, but, then, he didn't deny it, either.'

'And your attempt to get witnesses second time round failed.'

'That's because I was stupid enough to let him know I was on to him.'

'Anyway, there must be far easier ways than that for a crooked politician to make money, safer too. Not that he needs to, either. Rupert took a deliberate decision, he told me so himself, not to go into politics until he'd made

124

enough in the City to be completely self-sufficient. He's got all the money in the world. How much do you think that party cost that he gave last night?'

'He could be doing it for the kicks, I suppose,' I suggested lamely.

'A sort of Raffles, the Gentleman Cracksman? Unlikely. No, I'm sorry, Derek, it's all far too circumstantial, you must see that.'

'Yes, but he did try to kill me in the Members' Race, and what about that gang last night? They sound exactly like the lot who beat up the terrier-men. And you yourself— '

'Oh, I'm not saying Rupert wouldn't be up to every dirty trick there is, if he thought it worth his while. Some of his dealings in the City were pretty ruthless, I'm told. And I have no doubt at all that he found your interest in him embarrassing. But . . . hardly blackmail.'

'Why the attack last night, then?'

'That's easy. Warning you off to prevent you from getting too close to him. It won't be the first time that suspecting a man of one crime has led to the discovery of another.'

'Another?'

'We've had a tip-off that he's planning a political coup,' she said.

I stared at her.

'What sort of coup? Overthrowing the Government by force?'

'I suppose so. The informant didn't have any details.'

'But . . . that's impossible,' I said. 'Here, in this country!'

'That's what *we* thought. Rupert Massingham of all people. It sounded so ridiculous that we didn't even have the face to report it to our political masters. But the source wasn't one of the usual run of paid informers. It came from a professional thief, the sort of man who would have gone to prison for years – to the grave, even – sooner than grass on even his worst enemy. Said he felt he had to tell us for patriotic reasons and, oddly enough, whatever I thought about the rest of his story, I believed him in that.'

'So that made the story at least worth checking.'

'Yes, and I was given the job of finding out what I could by getting as close to him as possible. That presented no problem with Rupert, given any sort of looks. But I thought it was crazy at the time.'

'And now?'

'And now . . . I'm not so sure. I know so little about the political side; that's why I was so interested to hear that you were a Whip. I knew that Rupert had taken sudden exception to you and I wondered whether someone on high politically hadn't got wind of the same thing quite separately and put you on to it.'

'Only to find out that all I was doing was indulging in a spot of apparently misdirected private enterprise?'

'You could say that.'

Camberley's grin took my mind off the matter in hand, although it was only for a moment.

'But surely . . . he'd have to be an outright extremist even to consider a thing like that. I've always considered Rupert's place in the political spectrum as medium-to-wet.'

'I don't know. I'll tell you one thing, though. I've found out enough about Rupert already to know that, if anyone could do it, *he* could.'

'So what do we do about it?'

'Well, we've both arrived at something of a dead end. You're inhibited from taking the blackmail thing any further – even if it were worth doing in the context of Rupert – by your promise to this mystery friend of yours?'

I nodded.

'And I can't very well go back to him after the way

he walked out on me last night. I would like a shot if I thought it would do any good, but he'd be bound to be suspicious if I did. And the one really important thing as far as I'm concerned is to keep my cover, so I think the best thing—'

'But isn't that rather blown anyway? Ralph and his pals are bound to tell Rupert what you did to them.'

Camberley shook her head. 'Would *you*, in the circumstances? That's not to say that they won't come back and have another go at you on their own account. Perhaps the sooner we start on that coaching I suggested the better, tomorrow suit you?'

'Fine.'

'No, what I was going to suggest is that we should let it be known that we're going out together. Only temporarily of course, but that way I'd still come across him from time to time.' Her lips formed themselves into that slightly twisted look again. 'Or might that be an embarrassment to you?'

I thought for a moment. Julia still hadn't come back to the house when I had left for the office at nine o'clock. Even if she were to later in the day, I still owed her something for going off with Rupert, however innocent her behaviour thereafter might turn out to have been. I looked at Camberley, that glorious hair of hers, those wide enquiring eyes, the mouth. . . .

'I think I could bear it,' I said.

'Right, then. Is there anything else you've found out about Rupert that might be useful?'

'Hold on.' I searched back in my memory, particularly to the lunch at White's with Jimmy McKay. 'Well, he got a degree in engineering when he left Eton. His father and grandfather were both engineers; apparently his grandfather was the Massingham of Massingham Bridge fame – the thing tanks carried to help them over rough country in the First World War. But presumably he dropped

127

all that when he went into the City to prepare for his political career. That's all, I'm afraid.'

'I didn't know that.' Camberley made a note on her pad, 'worth bearing in mind, I suppose.' But she said it without a great deal of conviction. 'Now, tell me about the tunnel and exactly where you think it is, that really could be important.'

I got out the street-atlas of London and showed her the approximate site of the warehouse, the point at which I had seen the BMW disappear into it and the place where it had reappeared among the traffic coming from the left at the far side of Vauxhall Bridge.

'It didn't seem to have a great deal of relevance to blackmail,' I said, 'but I do see that, if you're planning something like your informant has in mind, having some means of getting from one side of the river to the other quickly that nobody knows about could be a different matter.'

Camberley nodded. 'Now, you work in politics. I know it's unlikely, but would you have any idea just how feasible a coup of some kind might be in this country?'

'Off-hand not the slightest, but I could certainly find out for you.' One of the advantages of working in the House of Lords is that one really can find an expert there on any conceivable subject.

'Could you do it this afternoon? While I look into the possibilities of the tunnel?'

'I'll do my best. It might just be worth checking into the ownership of the red Ford Fiesta used for the second lot of blackmail money, though.'

I gave it to her.

I knew that the police would have had it from Cully already, but I still wasn't prepared to relinquish any idea of Rupert Massingham being involved in the blackmailing of Dorothy, without giving it at least one more try.

* * *

128

The library of the House of Lords consists of a series of interconnecting rooms in which gothic elegance combines with comfort and linenfold panelling, bindings of calf and morocco and formal writing-tables set off deep red-leather armchairs. It was against this background that I found Lord Appleby immersed in the strip-cartoon page of the *Daily Mirror*. He was a long thin man, with a pronounced stoop and dark-rimmed spectacles, and always reminded me of a praying mantis.

He laid his newspaper aside as I approached him.

'The precious stone of erudition has many facets,' he remarked cheerfully. 'What can I do for you, Derek?'

Master of one of the leading Cambridge colleges, he was also a fellow of All Souls, Oxford, and probably the foremost living authority on English constitutional law.

I had given some thought as to how I could possibly introduce the subject without sounding particularly silly.

'Look, Sam,' I said, 'I'm writing a paper on the House of Lords in its rôle as a constitutional safeguard – you know, the right to prevent the House of Commons from prolonging its own life beyond the five-year period, that sort of thing – and I've come up against a bit of a problem. What would be the chances of some sort of political coup taking place in this country which could make any such parliamentary powers ineffective?'

I needn't have worried. He clearly regarded my question as a perfectly valid academic exercise and approached it as such. He paused for a moment in thought.

'Well, political coups do happen. They're most common in African and South American states but, in those cases, it usually only means replacing one totalitarian régime with another, and all the necessary machinery's already in place for the new controller to use. Of course the military there have long played a rôle that is far removed from that of their counterparts in the United Kingdom or, indeed, most European countries.'

'It happened in Russia,' I said.

'Yes, but there the various revolutions were able to take over the reins from what was virtually an absolute monarchy. Even in the satellite countries, the communist régimes succeeded fascist ones that were more or less tailor-made for them.'

'What about the original fascist governments, then, between the wars?'

'Ah, those were different. Mussolini was invited by King Victor Emmanuel to form a government, and the process was entirely constitutional. Hitler, again, became Chancellor in accordance with the law, formally appointed by Chancellor Hindenberg, and this legitimacy was a great asset to both dictators. Hitler was able to carry out the enabling decrees that virtually gave him absolute power by a legitimate vote in the Reichstag. Once you're in power, it becomes very much easier to take the steps necessary to retain it – and that would present fewer difficulties in the United Kingdom than in most countries, given our lack of a written constitution. It's getting there, the initial coup, that would be the problem.'

'But could it happen here? Under present conditions?'

'It would be a very rash man who said categorically that it couldn't.' Sam Appleby stooped even lower in his chair until his chin was resting in both hands.

Then he went on: 'It would involve the physical removal of the Prime Minister from Downing Street and other members of the Cabinet from their offices, their replacement by new men and the seizure of the principal means of communication – television, radio and the Press. There'd have to be a pretty bad state of affairs as a precondition, massive unemployment, economic collapse, breakdown of law and order, far worse than any of them is at the moment.

Even so, I very much doubt if it would ultimately come about without some other unforeseen and quite extraneous factor also having arisen.'

'Such as what?'

Sam shrugged his hunched shoulders. 'Wars or rumours of wars, perhaps. Some really devastating political scandal. Who knows? You'd need the support and active involvement of the Army or the Police of course, preferably the police in peacetime, but probably both. After that you'd have to pass the sort of emergency regulations that you had at the beginning of the last war, prolong the life of Parliament if it was still in existence – that's where the House of Lords would come in.' He paused. 'And then there's always the position of the Crown. . . . '

'Will you start or shall I?' said Camberley, as we met at the prearranged time that evening.

'You, please.'

'All right, then. There are twelve tunnels under the River Thames in Greater London. Two of them have been closed to the public since the beginning of the century: the Tower Subway and that which once served the old City and South London Railway. Five more form part of the London Underground Railway system. . . . '

Camberley ran through the list with the practised ease of a saying-lesson.

'A lot of them are in pairs of course, to cater for two-way traffic simultaneously, but I've counted them as one. Then there are a dozen or so service tunnels, electricity, gas, etc., but a man couldn't even walk down some of those, so I haven't counted them at all. Effectively, there are those twelve.'

'And mine isn't one of them?'

'And yours isn't one of them,' she said. 'I went to see the warehouse myself – I arranged a semi-official visit with

131

a colleague of mine in the area. It's built of sandlime bricks and probably put up' – she glanced at her notebook – 'some forty to forty-five years ago. There's an entrance at each end which you can't see from the road, but the wall that faces you is rock-solid, strengthened with brick piers twelve feet apart – that's another pointer to its age apparently, shortage of steel in wartime – no opening of any kind in it, not even a door that could have concealed one.'

'Well, yes,' I said. 'That was how it seemed to me when I went back on the following day.'

'But the really clinching factor is this. How far would you say the front of that warehouse is from the river?'

'Oh, I don't know. Forty or fifty yards perhaps?'

'Fifty-seven! A tunnel under the river at that point would have to be at least a hundred feet deep. You couldn't have a gradient steeper than one in ten for a car to get down, and that would be stretching it, so the entrance to such a tunnel would probably have to be at least half a mile back. And it's still got to have somewhere to come out north of the river. Here's the page in the street-atlas covering that area, and where could it possibly do that?'

'I do see the difficulty.'

'But I didn't leave it there. The river's about five hundred yards wide at that point and, for a tunnel that would take a car even of the size of a BMW, the amount of earth or clay that would have to be moved would be enormous. Something in the order of ten thousand tons, and you just couldn't carry out an operation of that size without at least someone knowing about it. Furthermore I'm told that the cost of it would be at least two million pounds in present-day terms. It would have to have been built for some specific purpose, and who could possibly have a use for such a tunnel that could justify expenditure like that?'

'I'm sorry, I seem to have wasted your time.'

'Never mind. It was a lead that had to be followed up. How did you get on?'

I gave her a pretty-well verbatim account of everything that Lord Appleby had said to me.

'The short answer is that any politician who was strong enough to sustain a political coup once it had happened would have been able to gain power far more easily by constitutional means in the first place.'

Camberley was silent for a moment or two.

Then: 'Oh, by the way, that red Ford Fiesta belongs to a man in Basingstoke who reported it stolen there, that same evening. Perhaps we'd better meet again tomorrow morning to decide where, if anywhere, we go from here.' Suddenly I got the full benefit of the grin, tooth and all. 'There goes my coup and your tunnel . . . *at a stroke*!' she said.

When I got back home late that evening the house felt different somehow, its atmosphere strange and unreal, and for quite some moments I stood there trying to work out why.

It was only when I went up to the bedroom that I realised what it was. The dressing-table that had been Julia's was bare, her wardrobe empty. Downstairs in the drawing-room again, the table that she had liked to work or read at was devoid of books and papers, her clothes, shoes, hats, jewellery, ornaments, the imprint of her personality even, had all vanished. There wasn't a single trace of her remaining – it was almost as though she had never been there at all.

And then I saw that there was one.

There on the drawing-room mantelpiece, left lying by itself as a sort of symbol, was the signet ring that had been my father's, which for the past eighteen months Julia herself had worn on the third finger of her right hand.

I picked it up and looked at the crest that was engraved on it, my own crest – that of the Mallicent family. An owl sitting on a velvet cap wearing a jagged collar round its neck and holding in its beak three roses on a single stalk, the whole surmounted by a viscount's coronet. And as I turned it listlessly over and over between my fingers its official heraldic description – 'On a Chapeau Sable turned up Ermine an owl Argent gorged dancetty Sable wings displayed Argent holding in its beak a Spray of three Roses Gules barbed, seeded, stalked and leaved proper' – kept running like a nursery jingle through my mind.

Suddenly, in spite of all the argument and unhappiness that had beset Julia and myself, I knew for an absolute certainty how desperately I was going to miss her. I put the ring on to the little finger of my own left hand. I wanted to be sure of having it immediately available if ever, in the future, there should be a chance of persuading her to take it back.

VIII

CASTING AGAIN

Wednesday, 19 March

' "Forcible removal of the Prime Minister and other members of the Cabinet from office; seizure of the principal means of communication; active support and involvement of the Armed Forces and the Police." I know it sounds ridiculous,' said Camberley, 'but let's just consider the possibilities a little further, rather than dismissing it out of hand. Where do we start?'

She and I had again met in my office at nine-thirty that morning.

'With the Police, first,' I said. 'Rupert really wouldn't be able to get anywhere without their at least turning a blind eye to it. You'd be in a position to know as well as anyone – could you ever conceive of them being prepared to countenance a thing like that?'

'Well, we're all worried sick about the law and order issue of course, but. . . . ' Camberley thought for a moment. Then she shook her head. 'No, it certainly hasn't got anywhere near as bad as that yet,' she said.

'How would he set about persuading them? If and when he did try.'

'There are various organisations that represent the interests of the police and their views generally, at different levels –

through them, I suppose. The top one's the Association of Chief Police Officers, made up of Chief Constables, their Assistants and Deputies – he'd need to get them on his side for a start. Then there's the Superintendents' Association of England and Wales; and finally the Police Federation, which goes down to the constable on the beat. They all hold their annual conferences in the autumn, and it isn't unknown for a minister to be invited to address them.'

'Yes, but only Home Office ministers, surely? Very few Cabinet ministers are prepared to put up with colleagues from other departments poaching on their own sphere of influence.'

'I suppose so.'

'No, my guess is that you'd actually have to be Home Secretary to achieve any worthwhile results in that direction,' I said. 'Or Secretary of State for Defence, as far as the Army's concerned. And Rupert's still a long way short of either of those – thank God.'

'Hold on, Rupert's a Treasury minister. Couldn't he get the support of the Police by a dramatic increase in expenditure on men, equipment and conditions of service – the Army, too, for that matter.'

'I doubt it. He could if he were Chancellor of the Exchequer, I suppose. Or Chief Secretary to the Treasury even – he's specifically in charge of all matters of supply. A strong Chief Secretary could possibly over-ride the Chancellor.'

'Rupert's strong enough.'

'Yes, but he's only Financial Secretary. The other two are in the Cabinet, and he's outside it. Not even Rupert could bridge that.'

Camberley looked at her watch. 'Well, I suppose I'd better go and report progress, such as it is, to my superior officer. There's no doubt at all that Rupert's up to something, though. Can I give you a lift anywhere, Derek?'

'No, thanks. I'm going to walk across the bridge and visit Tom and Ted in hospital. I never got a chance to, yesterday.'

I had been every day since the fight on Clapham Common, otherwise. Tom was more and more optimistic every time I saw him, but the doctor warned me not to hope too much. Ted was holding his own, just – and that was all he would say.

'Fine. But don't forget our lesson later; I've got the police gymnasium booked at— '

Just at that moment one of the telephones on the desk rang. I picked up the receiver.

'Lord Thyrde? Lady Elton for you. I didn't want to disturb you, but she says it's urgent.'

'Right, put her on,' I said resignedly.

'Derek?'

'Hello.'

'Can you . . . can you spare me a few minutes? Here? Something rather peculiar's happened, and I don't want to say anything over the telephone.'

'I'll come right round,' I said.

I put down the receiver and looked across the desk at Camberley.

'That', I said, 'was my blackmailee again. Didn't sound too bad, but I thought at the time that it was all a bit too good to be true for it to end quite so easily. I say, you don't suppose your informant jumped to the wrong conclusion in the first place, do you – heard about Rupert being involved in something, knew he was a politician, that sort of thing – and it's really blackmail all the time?'

'No, I don't think so,' Camberley said.

But I couldn't help feeling that she wasn't quite so sure about it now.

Dorothy Elton was smiling when she opened the door of her flat to me.

'Don't say a word, Derek, until you've seen what I've got to show you.'

She took me by the hand, led me into the drawing-room and over to the grand piano that stood to the right of the window.

'There, now.' She pointed to the briefcase that lay conspicuously, by itself, on the polished walnut top. 'Open it. It's not locked.'

I did as I was told.

'Where ... what ...?' There was no doubt about it. It was the same briefcase that I had given to Tom through the window of my car nine days before, and there inside it were the bundles of notes, each in its red plastic band. I picked one of them up and riffled its edges.

'It's all there. Ten thousand pounds. I've counted it.'

'But how ...?' I said.

'Twenty minutes ... half an hour ago. Just like I found the papers on Monday, I opened the door and there it was just outside. No laundry-box this time, today's Wednesday. I took it inside and opened it up. I still had the combination. I couldn't believe it at first, just looked at it ... and looked at it. And then I rang you.'

'But what an extraordinary thing to happen.'

She nodded. 'Isn't it, just? But oh, Derek, I am so glad you've got your money back.'

'Hold on a minute,' I said. 'You've lost fifty thousand pounds. You must have this.'

Her chin jutted forward.

'No.'

'All right, then, we'll share it. Your fifty to my ten, that means I take a sixth of it. Let me see. . . .' I did a rapid mental calculation. 'You give me one thousand, six hundred and sixty-six pounds of it, and I'll let you off the odd point six six recurring,' I said.

138

'No, don't you see, Derek? By forfeiting that fifty thousand I feel that I've paid the price for what poor George and I did all those years ago. If I took it back now, any of it, I'd somehow be reneging on him. No, you must have it, it's yours – I think they're the same notes even.'

I took out my diary and compared the numbers which I had jotted down in it with the notes in one of the bundles.

'Yes, they are,' I said.

'Now I really can forget the whole thing – for ever. And I've got something else here for you,' she smiled, 'by way of interest.'

She walked over to the table by her chair on the right-hand side of the fireplace and brought back from it one of those little blue-cardboard jeweller's boxes which she handed to me.

I opened it. It was a tie-pin, a running fox in tiny gem diamonds, no more than half an inch long and only in outline but totally expressive of movement – the nicest that I had ever seen.

'It's lovely,' I said, 'it really is, but I can't take it.' And I thrust it back at her before the temptation to accept became too much for me.

But she put it firmly into my hand again and closed my fingers round it.

'It was George's. I want you to have it, Derek. It will be a thank-you from him, too,' she said.

It was a bright windy cheerful morning as I strode across Westminster Bridge, still carrying with me the uplift from the changed atmosphere in which I had left Dorothy and conscious, although I couldn't see it, of the enchanting new running fox which was already adorning one of the dark blue stripes of my Brigade tie.

139

I rounded the corner by St Thomas' and recognised the familiar figure walking towards me while it was still some forty or fifty yards away.

'Hello, Cully,' I said.

Something was wrong; his eyes were staring straight ahead, unfocused – unseeing even.

I touched him on the arm as he passed by. 'Cully?'

He stopped, gave a couple of brisk shakes to his shoulders, turned slowly and looked at me.

'Hello, m'Lord.'

'Is it Ted?' I said gently.

'Ted? No, Ted's conscious again. Coming along nicely, is Ted.' He paused. 'Tom. . . . '

'Tell me.'

'Tom's heart stopped sudden, see? Pul . . . pulmomonary embolism, they called it. Clot in the blood, like.'

I ought to have foreseen at least the possibility, I suppose, the warnings had all been there, but this sudden descent from carefreeness into tragedy, the immediate sense of personal loss, the knowledge that I myself had been directly responsible left me for several seconds incapable of saying anything.

'When did it happen?' I said at last.

'He were took bad this morning. Horspital done all they could; two hour they was at it. Weren't no hope, though.'

'Cully, I *am* sorry.' I searched for words of more practical comfort, but none came. 'Would it be all right for me to go in and see Ted, then?'

'You do that, m'Lord. I dursen't. He don't know about Tom yet, see? Tell it from the way I were looking, would Ted.' He paused and his features formed themselves into an expression the like of which I had never before seen on that kind and gentle face. 'That there Massingham! You let me know when you need more help with him, Derek.'

140

'Of course I will,' I said, although I had long since made up my mind that nothing would induce me ever again to involve the Terrier-men in such an enterprise, 'but it seems that there's just a chance now it wasn't Rupert Massingham after all.'

Cully shook his head.

'Don't you fret, it were him all right.' And without a further word he walked off along the pavement in the spring sunshine. I stood there and watched him until he disappeared round the corner and out of sight, in the direction from which I had come.

Then, with a feeling of total emptiness inside me, I went on into St Thomas' Hospital to pay my planned visit to Ted.

'Bad as that, was she?' said Camberley, the moment she saw my face on arrival. 'What's the new development?'

I shook my head. 'Nothing to do with the blackmail this time; that really does seem to be over.' And I told her about Tom.

She laid a hand on my shoulder for a moment or two. Then 'Come on, Derek, let's get changed,' was all she said.

I soon found out that in her wisdom Camberley had devised a therapy far more effective than any mere words of sympathy could have provided. For the next twenty minutes she put me through a workout that didn't allow me time for thought even, let alone any for brooding. Muscles that I seemed to have acquired new for the occasion were beginning to assert themselves with a precocity that was decidedly out of place.

We had the gymnasium to ourselves, a room some twenty yards by thirty; a thick wrestling-mat covered three-quarters of the floor area and, apart from the horizontal wooden bars that lined the walls, the only other piece of equipment was a leather-topped vaulting-horse that stood by itself, sad and neglected, in one corner. She was wearing a dark green leotard moulded to that superb figure of hers and a matching sweat-band restraining the glorious russet hair, the colour setting off both it and the creamy white of her bare limbs to perfection.

I learnt how to fall properly. The elementary movements in self-defence that she taught me included some of those that she had already described to me in the restaurant on Monday evening. Only when she was satisfied that I was proficient enough in one of them to stand at least a chance of carrying it out in real earnest did she allow me to move on to the next.

'We'll try the bit with the knife man now,' she said. 'I'll do it to you first to give you the idea. Here's your knife.' She passed me a rolled-up copy of the *Evening Standard*. 'Right then, you're going to be the villain so, to make it anything like convincing, we'll have to get you into the right frame of mind.'

Suddenly her voice hardened.

'Look at you,' she said, 'you've been made to look a bloody fool in front of your two friends, and by a woman, too, yes, I know they've been knocked out themselves since, but they're sure to blame that on you afterwards; you've just been kicked in the balls, it's still hurting like hell and at the back of your mind you've got that fear, instinctive to all males, that it might have damaged you permanently in some way; you're on your own now . . . you've still got a chance, just this one, of getting your own back and regaining at least a certain amount of your self-respect; there in your hand is the means of carrying it out and you don't give a damn for the consequences, so come at me with that knife, plunge it into me anywhere . . . Come on, come on, then . . . NOW!'

I didn't stand a chance. I hadn't expected to really, but it all happened so quickly. There was I lying knifeless, flat on

142

my back on the mat, gawping foolishly at the ceiling; and then there was Camberley, hand outstretched and grinning at my discomfiture, helping me to my feet.

She picked up the rolled newspaper from where it had fallen.

'All right, now it's your turn,' she said. 'We'll take it a step at a time. I'll explain to you exactly what to do at each stage, and you repeat the gist of it back to me as you do it. That way, it will stick in your mind.'

I stood there waiting, my hands hanging loosely down by my sides.

'No, that's wrong for a start. Hold your hands up level with your face, like this.'

'*Hands raised*,' I said.

'Here I come, then.' Camberley pointed the rolled paper towards my midriff and walked slowly towards me. 'The first thing for you to do is to minimise the target area. Pivot on your left heel and move your right foot back and sideways, so that your body is at right angles to mine.'

'*Pivot on left heel, right foot back and sideways, thereby reducing target area.*'

'Good. As the knife comes forward, drop your right hand on to mine, the assailant's, taking care to avoid the weapon of course, and grip it as hard as you can so as to immobilise my fingers.'

'*Drop right hand on to assailant's, avoiding weapon, and grip to immobilise fingers.*'

'Now, as I come forward propelled by my own impetus, spin my hand round so that the palm is uppermost, put your left arm under mine, the assailant's, right grabbing your own wrist so as to form a wrist-lock, then force your right hand down and your left arm up, the resultant pain causing me, the assailant, first, to drop the weapon . . . .'

'*Spin hand round so that palm uppermost, my left arm under*

143

assailant's right, grab own wrist, force right hand down, left arm up, causing assailant first drop weapon . . . ' The rolled-up newspaper fell to the mat.

' . . . and, second, to arch my body forward. Now, drive your right knee into my solar plexus. Do that bit gently, if you don't mind.'

'Then, as body arches forward, right knee into solar plexus.'

'And there you are.' She got up from the mat. 'Right, we'll try it for real now.'

It took something like ten times before Camberley was satisfied and, in the process, I found out just how hard a rolled-up newspaper can be when one fails to minimise the target – or does it just too late.

But at the eleventh attempt everything went according to instructions – or almost. There was Camberley, face up on the mat as I had been, but at the last moment, totally exhausted, I lost my balance and collapsed on top of her, only just managing to put out my hands in time to avoid squashing her flat.

'Clever boy! I'm not sure whether that's *quite* the way we should have ended up, but I really think you're getting the idea at last.'

There was a sheen from recent exertion on the moulded curves of her pink and white face, and the violet depths of those eyes only an inch or so from mine hinted at possibilities for the future. My gaze passed from them to the damp mouth still parted in a smile, and I lowered my lips to hers, warm, soft and, after a moment's hesitation, welcoming. I kissed her for a long long time.

When I raised my head again, Camberley's wide innocent eyes were looking up into mine almost speculatively.

'You do realise', she said, 'that I could break your back from this position?'

'Why don't you, then?'

144

There was a pause, as though she were actually giving the suggestion serious consideration.

Then 'I don't know. Somehow I've got a feeling that it might be rather a waste,' she said.

The room occupied by the Leader of the House of Lords is one of the most aesthetically pleasing in the whole Palace of Westminster. Designed as a bedroom for early-Victorian Lords Chancellor, the intricate moulding of frieze and ceiling has been gilded and decorated in the spirit of Pugin's original concept and, although the motif of the hand-blocked wallpaper incorporates lilies, roses and thistles, the effect is restful rather than sumptuous, giving an overall impression of muted browns and blues. Summoned to it later that afternoon by a harassed messenger, I opened the door with a certain amount of trepidation and this was by no means diminished when I saw that my immediate superior, the Earl of Lavenham – Chief Whip of the House of Lords and Captain of the Gentlemen-at-Arms – was already there sitting in one of the off-white covered armchairs by the window.

'Ah, Derek, come in and sit down,' said Lord Oldfield from the sofa in the middle and he indicated the other armchair with a wave of his hand.

I did so.

'Now, the first thing I've got to tell you is that I've had a letter from James Banbury telling me that his doctors have ordered him complete rest for the next six months and he's come to the conclusion that the only fair thing for him to do is to resign from his office of Deputy Chief Whip and Captain of the Yeomen of the Guard. Tom here recommends, and I agree with him, that I should put your name forward to the Prime Minister as a replacement for James. If you've no objection, that is?'

The whole room started revolving slightly. I had been absolutely certain in my own mind that I'd been summoned there to be sacked from the Front Bench altogether. I looked from one to the other.

'Thank you very much,' I said.

'That's settled, then. The next thing is rather less pleasant, I'm afraid. I've been talking to Tom about what happened up at Mathersdon on Saturday. You'll have read about that of course.'

'Er. . . . '

I intercepted a fleeting glance of exasperation, cast by Patrick in the direction of his Chief Whip.

'Don't you *ever* read the newspapers, Derek?' Tom Lavenham said good-naturedly. 'Those anti-nuclear demonstrations that got out of hand.'

'Good Lord, yes,' I said. I'd heard about them vaguely of course, but my mind had been on other things since.

'There was a crowd of some five thousand there,' said Patrick, 'and the thing started peaceably enough. Then, suddenly and quite uncharacteristically, it developed into a riot. They think the whole thing was stirred up by troublemakers brought in from outside, but the net result was that quite a lot of policemen were injured, some of them seriously, and at least four others were killed – one an unfortunate passer-by who didn't have anything to do with the demonstration at all.'

'How did it end?'

'Well, it seems that at that point the local Chief Constable, entirely on his own initiative, brought in USCRODD, the new crowd-dispersal device – that's not public knowledge yet. The only good thing to come out of the whole business is that apparently it worked like a charm.'

'But didn't Peter White . . . ?'

'That's the whole point. You were at Home Affairs the day the matter was first discussed. Can you remember the exact words he used? I've got the minutes here, but they're not quite clear on that point.'

'Something along the lines that he was going to give a personal undertaking in private to his Labour opposite number that wouldn't commit the whole Government, only himself and so long as he was Home Secretary.'

Patrick nodded grimly. 'That was my recollection, too. Apparently Jonathon Finchley, the Shadow Home Secretary, has got wind of what happened, and Peter insists that he's going to resign over it. The question now is whether the Prime Minister should accept his resignation or not.'

'What do you think?' I asked.

'Well, there are other factors to be taken into consideration, too, of course. Those four deaths could have been avoided and our own party, certainly the right wing of it, will be up in arms over him ever having given such an undertaking in the first place. Then there's the Chief Constable himself to be taken into consideration and that particular man is among the best we've got as well as being far and away the most popular. Nothing must be done to prejudice his position. No, my own view is that Peter will have to go, and what you've just told me confirms it.'

He was silent for a moment or two.

'Ironic really. The rest of us were every bit as responsible for the decision. Well, with the exception of Rupert Massingham, of course, yet it's Peter who suffers for it.' He looked at me closely. 'As I remember it, you supported Rupert at the time. Why was that?'

'Only that everything that could go wrong for the Conservatives seemed to be doing so and I thought it would be tempting providence to take one more risk of that happening, however slight.'

'Oh.' It was clear that Patrick Oldfield considered what I had said to be too frivolous to be worth further comment.

147

'Well, that's politics for you, I suppose. Tragedy, though, that such a promising career should have to end like that.'

As to that, I was in two minds myself. The violence was horrific of course, and it was certainly bad luck on poor Peter White, but it did occur to me that it might be no bad thing for the office of Secretary of State for Home Affairs to become vacant just at that moment. It was the one Cabinet post that John Elton had always wanted and this might be the very incentive needed to bring him back into active politics, where he was so badly needed, by accepting the candidature of Gloucestershire East.

'Incidentally, Derek, you remember talking to me about Rupert Massingham some weeks ago. Do you still hold those rather startling views of yours about him?'

Tom Lavenham glared warningly at me. But I was having serious doubts about the whole thing myself, particularly with regard to the blackmailing of Dorothy. And in any case, with my renewed promise to her at Rupert's party, I was now doubly inhibited from giving the slightest substantiation to what I had hinted at.

I shook my head.

'It all seemed pretty convincing at the time, but I've come to the conclusion that I must have got it wrong,' I said.

Back in my own office, I was sitting and taking a meditative look at the surroundings that would be mine in my own right from now on, when the telephone rang.

'Derek? Jimmy McKay here. Can you come and have lunch with me tomorrow?'

'Hold on, I'll look in my diary. Yes, I'd love to,' I said.

'Fine.' He named the time and the restaurant. 'Seen the tape, have you?'

'No,' I said. Something or other arising from Mathersdon, I supposed.

'The Gloucestershire East Conservatives have announced their candidate for the by-election. The Chief Whip's moving the writ in the House tomorrow.'

'Who is it?'

I held my breath. Literally.

'Young Tony Millard. You remember, the fellow who was narrowly beaten by the SDP last October.' There was a pause. 'Pity. I'm afraid this really does mean John Elton's out of politics for good,' he said.

IX

HUIC HOLLOA

Thursday, 20 March to Thursday, 2 October

'What about the new Home Secretary, then?' said Jimmy McKay.

He had avoided choosing any of those currently fashionable restaurants where the main course consists, at exorbitant cost, of a couple of slivers of culinary exotica, accompanied by a tea-plate of plain under-boiled vegetables in Technicolor greens and oranges. We had gone instead to a more reactionary establishment, where quantity matched quality for those who wanted it and food looked and tasted as one has always dreamt it to be. My knife had just sunk into a Tournedos Rossini, the oozing redness of which could have inspired a Turner sunset, and the Château Talbot that complemented it to perfection was of a silken smoothness.

They lost my attention forthwith.

'Er. . . . '

He laughed. 'Don't worry, Derek, I'm not trying to trap you into an indiscretion. It's common knowledge that Peter White's resigning and, as to who's going to replace him, that's a foregone conclusion. I'm told it's going to be announced this afternoon anyway.'

'You've got the advantage of me there,' I said. 'But,

150

assuming that you *are* right about Peter, who do you reckon would get the job?'

'You mean you really don't know?' Jimmy refilled his glass from the bottle of Cousin Louisa on the table. 'Yet another in the long line of embarrassments for the Government and, with a top Cabinet minister involved this time, probably the most damaging so far. Work it out for yourself, Derek. Who's the one man in your party who's never put a foot wrong?'

I put down my knife and fork.

'Not . . . Rupert?'

Suddenly I realised what must have lain behind the apparently innocuous question that Patrick Oldfield had asked me about Rupert Massingham just before I had left his room the day before. Obviously I had managed to instil into Patrick's mind enough of a doubt about Rupert for him to feel the need of satisfying himself on the latter's fitness to hold down one of the top Government positions and, like a fool, I had succeeded in dispelling rather than fostering it. It probably wouldn't have made a lot of difference in the end, but I could at least have tried.

'Only thing they can do, in the circumstances. It's a big jump, of course, Financial Secretary to Secretary of State for Home Affairs, but one of that order is not entirely without precedent.' Jimmy's eyes were half-shut as usual, but I wasn't in the least deceived by the almost total lack of expression on his face. 'You don't like him, do you?'

'Not very much,' I said. 'Would you, in my position?'

'You know what I mean.'

I had known, actually. Jimmy McKay would never have alluded to Julia's departure, especially in terms like that, unless I had first brought up the subject myself. And I was rapidly getting the impression that his political antennae had begun to pick up rather more than static as far as Rupert was concerned.

'If I ever do get wind of anything in that direction, I'll keep you posted,' he said.

I saw Rupert himself coming out of Patrick Oldfield's room later that afternoon. He was striding off past me down the dim red-carpeted corridor when I tapped him on the shoulder. He stopped and turned.

'Oh, it's you, Derek.'

'It seems I have to congratulate you,' I said.

There was a noticeable silence, and for a moment his eyes had lost both their intensity and their sparkle. Whether it was embarrassment over meeting me so soon after he had walked off with Julia like that, or whether Camberley had been right in her prediction that Ralph and his friends would have omitted to tell him about what had happened afterwards and it was merely surprise at seeing me relatively unscathed, I couldn't be certain. Probably the latter, because he peered forward and looked at me more closely.

'Bruised your face, dear?'

'Yes. Silly of me. I ran into a door,' I said.

'Ah, yes . . . well, thank you very much. I must confess that the Home Secretary's job is one that's always appealed to me, but I'd rather it hadn't been at the expense of poor old Peter. Still, you and I did our best at Home Affairs, didn't we?'

I was never quite sure to what extent anything that Rupert said could be taken at its face value and whether it didn't incorporate a sort of underlying facetiousness. The idea, for instance, that my poor efforts would have played any part at all in relation to his.

'You've heard about Tom Bannister?' I said.

'Yes, someone did mention it. You'll be going to the funeral, I suppose? You wouldn't like to represent me there, would you?'

'Don't you think you ought to go yourself?'

'Perhaps you're right. By the way, no hard feelings about Julia, I hope?'

I was damned if I was going to give him that satisfaction. And, in any case, I had come to the conclusion that Julia must have made up her mind to leave me already rather than Rupert having succeeded in luring her away – much though he had tried to.

'Er . . . no.'

Maddeningly, my thought processes must have been only too apparent to Rupert Massingham, because immediately he winked at me.

'That's the spirit, dear. Give my regards to Camberley,' he said.

Somewhat perversely, perhaps, in view of everything that had stemmed from my first sight of it, I had taken to driving in to Westminster by the route that led past the warehouse. As I did so on the following Tuesday, I noticed that the gates to the yard had been left open. I pulled over to the side of the road, got out of the car and looked in.

The wall of the warehouse lay solid and unbroken ahead of me, some twenty feet high and sixty yards long reinforced at twelve- or thirteen-foot intervals by the brick piers that Camberley had described to me, and from where I stood it was difficult to see now how I could possibly have imagined that there was any form of opening in it. A trick of the light and shade in that one fleeting glance caught through a chink in the wooden gates, a shadow thrown by the BMW perhaps? There seemed to be no one about, and there would certainly never be a better opportunity of knowing for certain, so I walked down the sloping yard and took a closer look.

The piers themselves, some two feet wide and fifteen inches deep, extended up to a couple of courses below the tile roof where they were protected against the weather by sloping caps of concrete at the top and both they and the wall they supported, painted long ago, had faded over the years to a soft and dirty pastel grey stippled with white in places. I walked along the face of it until I must have covered the place where I'd thought I'd seen the hole with the car disappearing into it, and there wasn't a sign of a crack even – save only at the point where, the brickwork rising from the concrete surface of the yard, little weeds had forced themselves through and marked the joint by a long, thin and almost continuous line of green.

The Chamber of the House of Commons was packed solid immediately after Prayers that afternoon, and below me I could see latecomers, according to the temperament of each of them, either urging their friends to squeeze up along the green-leather benches enough to free an uncomfortable inch or two for themselves or resignedly taking up a standing position at either end. I myself, there partly out of duty and partly, I had to confess, out of morbid interest, had been lucky enough to find a seat in the Peers' Gallery. The new Home Secretary was to be answering questions for the first time that day.

The first two questions, which were of purely local interest to the Member concerned, were answered by the Minister of State and a Parliamentary Secretary respectively. Then there was an audible stirring of excitement. I glanced down at the Order Paper with which I had provided myself on the way in.

To ask the Secretary of State for Home Affairs whether it remains the policy of his Department that the new crowd-dispersal device, known as USCRODD, will not be used in connection with anti-nuclear demonstrations.

'Mr Bradbury,' called the Speaker.

A tall fussy-looking man with pronounced grey side-whiskers, a fawn tweed suit and apple-green waistcoat stood up in his place on the front Opposition bench below the gangway.

'Number three, sir,' he said.

There was a low but swelling rumble of 'Hear, hear' from the Government benches together with, I thought I detected, an echo or two from those of the official Opposition and nobody could doubt the air of authority as, this time, Rupert Massingham rose quickly to his feet and laid his folder down on the Dispatch Box.

'No, sir,' he said and he resumed his seat.

The tall fussy-looking man jumped up, spluttering slightly.

'Mr Bradbury,' repeated the Speaker.

'Surely the Right Honourable Gentleman realis. .ses that the very es. .sence of the anti-nuclear movement is non-violence. Is he going to let one is. .olated inc. .cident influence him in this way?'

Rupert rose slightly more slowly.

'There may be something in what the Honourable Gentleman says, Mr Speaker, and until recently many of us would have agreed with him, but experience has shown that it really would not be in the public interest to lay down any hard and fast rules over this matter.'

Before he even had time to sit down this time, Members were on their feet in all parts of the House, including one at the Opposition Dispatch Box, the Shadow Home Secretary, who also happened to be the member of the Shadow Cabinet that I personally knew best.

'Mr Finchley,' said the Speaker.

There was the slightest of pauses before Jonathon Finchley put his question.

'Perhaps I can help the Right Honourable Gentleman, whose integrity and ability I know the whole House respects.

155

Would he perhaps be able to give an undertaking that, in whatever circumstances it may prove to be necessary to use USCRODD, it will only be done at the direct instigation of the Chief Constable concerned?'

Rupert gave a slight nod of his head in acknowledgement across the table before replying.

'I am afraid, Mr Speaker, that even such a limited undertaking might prove to be disastrous in certain circumstances. In the absence of the Chief Constable, I believe that it would be wholly wrong to deprive his deputy, one of his assistants or even some other police officer of relatively junior rank but who happened to be the senior officer present on a particular occasion, of what might prove to be the one means of avoiding serious injury and risk to life itself.'

Angry murmurs from across the floor of the House could be heard above the cheers of the Government benches, and these brought to his feet the Leader of the Opposition. Newly elected, he was as yet unproved in that position and clearly on the lookout for opportunities to make his mark.

'Mr Vane-Robertson.'

'That simply isn't good enough, Mr Speaker. Surely the Right Honourable Gentleman realises the extent of the disquiet felt by all sections of the community over the danger to democracy that the indiscriminate use of this device might represent?'

This time when Rupert rose to reply it was with an air of such compelling candour that even I found myself being convinced by it. He placed a hand on either side of the Dispatch Box, leant forward slightly and spoke into a silence that was almost tangible.

'I do of course, Mr Speaker, recognise the over-riding importance of preserving freedom of expression, together with the rights of minorities, and I can give the House this assurance that, just as soon as it becomes appropriate, with this in mind and with the advantage of experience, to lay down guidelines for the use of USCRODD, I shall not hesitate to do so.'

The murmur of approbation as Rupert Massingham sat down came with equal volume from all sides of the House. Even Mr Bradbury in the apple-green waistcoat was nodding his head.

Rupert answered three more questions himself, the remainder being taken by his subordinates. And when, at three-fifteen, someone got up and asked the Prime Minister the first of five identical questions – whether he would list his official engagements for Tuesday, 25 March – I reluctantly made my way out of the gallery. I was already overdue back in my place on the Lords' Front Bench.

Downstairs in the Commons Lobby I met Jonathon Finchley coming out of the Chamber for what must have been an equally pressing engagement. He was a cheerful gregarious man, instantly liked and rightly trusted by almost everybody.

'Hello, Derek. Come to hear your new star performing?'

'Yes,' I said. 'How did you think he got on?'

'Well enough. We could do with one or two like Rupert on our side,' he said.

And I repeated this to Camberley when she came out to dinner with me that evening.

'He's obviously just as much under the spell of Rupert Massingham as everyone else is,' I said, 'but I could see what he meant. Rupert had the whole House eating out of his hand, even the extreme Left.'

I had taken her to the only good restaurant at a reasonable distance from Westminster, because I was due to be summoned back to the House to vote at any time. I also told her about my unplanned visit to the warehouse that morning.

157

'So whatever the explanation about what I saw, or thought I saw, that morning it seems that you were right about that, too, and the tunnel probably doesn't exist, either.'

'Probably?' Camberley frowned at me from across the table, but she was looking more totally desirable than I had seen her yet. 'Don't you see, Derek, it simply *can't* exist. And, as for the other thing, who ever heard of a blackmailer yet who demanded money only to give it back?'

I nodded. None of it had done any more than confirm the conclusions that she and I had come to already, but it hadn't been any help to us in making up our minds as to what we were to do next, either. As for Rupert, whatever he *was* up to – and it must be something – he now seemed to be virtually unstoppable.

And it wasn't until dinner was over that Camberley gave me the worst news of all. She had been sitting opposite me for some moments in silence, holding her coffee-cup and gazing into the depths of it as though she were seeking inspiration from something hidden within.

'I've been trying to tell you and putting it off all evening somehow, but . . . I'm afraid this has got to be the end of our partnership,' she said.

'What do you mean?'

She looked up at me, her wide violet eyes troubled. 'They're taking me off the case. It's all too difficult, you see, now that Rupert's Home Secretary.'

'Does that mean that they don't suspect him any more, your lot?'

'No, at least, I don't think so. Someone far higher up than me will be handling it from now on, and then only very carefully. But, if ever you should get anything really concrete on Rupert, do still get in touch with me immediately and I will with you.'

'Yes, of course I will, but ... we can go on meeting for a meal or a drink sometimes? Can't we?'

She gave me a ravishing smile and reached forward across the table and gripped my hand.

'Yes, of course we can. I'd like that, if you want to.'

And the wretched waiter had to choose that particular moment to come up with the telephone message that I'd been expecting. The division in the House of Lords was imminent.

We walked out to my car together. She wouldn't go back to the House with me as I asked her to, but she did come into my arms and kiss me in a way that I'd been hoping that she would all evening.

It felt far too much like goodbye, all the same.

Over the weeks that followed, Camberley and I did manage to meet fairly regularly. She even gave me two more lessons at the police gymnasium, during which I was not only able to revise the movements that I had learnt on the first occasion to an extent that I was confident of being able to carry them out in earnest should the occasion arise, but also to progress to rather more sophisticated forms of self-defence as well. But, in spite of Camberley's forebodings, Ralph and his friends seemed to have decided against any form of retaliation in my direction and I was even rather disappointed when I realised that I wasn't going to be given the chance.

We also had a meal together from time to time, and Camberley was meticulous in insisting that she should be the host on alternate occasions. But it was usually lunch rather than dinner, and one or other of us always seemed to be in a rush to get away afterwards – she again working under cover, although as to the exact nature of her new assignment I was never to find out, and I finding my new duties as Deputy Chief Whip even more time-consuming, especially as we were now entering into the busiest time of the parliamentary year. These meetings were far rarer than I myself would have liked, but I was reluctant to press her any harder for fear that I might lose even that.

The only good thing to come out of it as far as I was concerned was that I soon came to know for certain that I had become totally immune to Julia Elton. As for Julia herself, from all that I heard she was still very much tied up with Rupert Massingham, although to what extent she was likely to allow whatever relationship existed between them to become permanent nobody I knew was prepared to venture an opinion. It was about time the silly bitch made up her mind as to what she really did want.

I still managed to find time to go and visit Ted Bannister, who was maintaining his recovery in hospital, on a fairly regular basis. While I missed Tom no less, I soon found myself liking Ted quite as much, although in a totally different way. Tom's more forthright manner of expressing himself had always overshadowed his brother, who was far less critical in his approach and prepared to make allowances for everybody – even, to Cully's manifest disgust, including Rupert Massingham – and reserve his final judgement on any possible defect in their character until it could be proved conclusively by subsequent actions or events.

While the economic situation and that of unemployment grew steadily worse, giving rise to promises of more and more extreme remedial measures by the wilder elements of the Opposition, the only improvement in the Government's fortunes was in the field of law and order. On two separate occasions, major operations undertaken by the police against drug-traffickers in different parts of the country were carried out immaculately, without developing into the sort of racially orientated riots that had become the hallmark of similar attempts in the recent past, while a regular series of demonstrations by the anti-nuclear movement had passed off as patterns of the restraint and orderliness that were claimed, and indeed intended, by their organisers. The former, I was told by Patrick Oldfield afterwards, had been entirely due to the judicious and timely use of USCRODD, whereas the latter emphatically had not.

Only once during the whole of that summer did I see, or even hear about, the new Home Secretary being at a disadvantage, and that was in June at the annual puppy show of the Yardley Hunt.

It was Tuesday, 24 June the day on which those people who had 'walked' last season's hound puppies, letting them wander at will about their farmyard or garden from about twelve weeks old until it was time at eighteen months for them to be taken into the discipline of the hunt kennels, came to see their own particular charges judged against others. Camberley, looking as lovely as ever, was with me, having for once been able to get away.

There was a challenge cup each for the best dog and bitch puppies and the best couple, to be kept for a year by their respective walkers. A small replica was theirs outright, and a silver-plated teaspoon engraved with the Yardley 'Y' was given as a memento to winners and losers alike. But primarily it was a day out for everybody with tea afterwards, a gesture of thanks from the Masters to all those who helped the Yardley Hunt throughout the year and not only in this traditional and indispensable way.

A square of rails put up to mark off the showing arena, banked chairs all round it for the spectators – the sun and the hats and the people. Every year, it was an afternoon of universal enjoyment. But this one was a puppy show that I shall remember all my life.

Rupert Massingham, in bowler hat and long white kennel-coat, was in the ring trying to show off Vandal, a doghound by Heythrop Muddler out of Yardley Valour – traditionally

161

names of hound puppies are chosen with the same initial letter as their dam – to best advantage. He was having a certain amount of difficulty, because Vandal's legs seemed to be made of indiarubber, splaying in all directions, and no amount of tempting with biscuit succeeded in coaxing him into the show position, head up, ears alert, hind feet back and stern out straight. There was a sound of tentative clapping among the onlookers which grew into a crescendo accompanied by full-bodied cheers and Rupert, pausing for a moment in his seemingly impossible task, looked up to see what it was.

Cully, with the conscious pride of a young mother showing off her new baby in its perambulator, was escorting Ted on elbow crutches through the chairs and the forest of arms held out by the occupants to welcome them. There was no word spoken, but the eyes of both were on Rupert, Cully's having assumed an expression of disgust and Ted's one of mild interest. They paused at the side of the ring.

For a moment the three of them formed an almost theatrical tableau until Rupert, unable to meet their combined gaze, glanced away, catching my eye as he did so. Immediately he spun round on his feet and, instead of tossing the bit of biscuit that he had been holding to Vandal as that unfortunate had been expecting, he threw it as hard as he could at his back, causing him to shy away with a yelp. Whether it was in anger at the Terrier-men, at himself because of his involuntary reaction or at me for having witnessed it, it was hard to say.

When Cully and Ted, who had also turned, came towards where Camberley and I were sitting, their faces lit up into a smile of recognition.

'Grand to see you here,' I said, gripping their hands. 'How are you both?'

Cully had clearly reverted to his accustomed rôle of silent leadership, because it was Ted who spoke.

'Cully and me's getting along famous, m'Lord, thanking you kindly. Same be. . . . ' his voice faltered, but it was only for a moment, 'same be we're always done,' he said.

The House of Commons rose for the Summer Recess on Friday, 25 July, and the Lords on Thursday, the 31st.

In the mean time, the Government's long run of accident-proneness was continuing unabated, and it seemed that scarcely a week went by without another instance of it arising. Three more junior ministers were forced to resign, one because he and his wife had gone on a long and expensive holiday that was subsequently discovered to have been funded by a company the profitability of whose activities depended to a large extent on the goodwill of his own Government department and one because he had become involved in a particularly unsavoury divorce case. The third had had to go simply because it had no longer been possible to overlook the fact that he just wasn't up to carrying out the duties for which he was paid.

In August the unemployment figures reached an all-time high. Interest rates rose dramatically. Inflation was at 5 per cent for the first time in two years and, increasingly, wage settlements were being made at over 10 per cent.

The official Opposition, who manifestly presented the only viable alternative to the present administration, had become more and more radical in their utterances and the undertakings that they were now making as to the way in which, if elected, they would deal with the situation showed all the characteristics of a potential one-party state. Their Leader, it was revealed by one of the newspapers, had been paying a series of surreptitious visits to Moscow, to discuss 'matters of mutual interest between potentially fraternal régimes'. And this, after one or two half-hearted efforts, the Party organisation gave up even trying to deny.

163

On the credit side, the one man who had been an exception to the Government's record of disasters even managed to improve his position. Under Rupert as Home Secretary, the new crowd-dispersal device was now being seen to be used with such skill and sensitivity that rioting could be dealt with far more economically and effectively than ever before. The moment any possibility of unrest arose, the police just whistled up USCRODD on their hand radios and everything became orderly again. They no longer had to attend demonstrations in large numbers and were able to revert to their proper rôle of combating crime, the incidence of which had started to fall dramatically. In the end, the troublemakers just stopped bothering to turn up at all.

Rupert Massingham, invited to address the annual general meetings of the Association of Chief Police Officers, the Superintendents' Association of England and Wales and the Police Federation, received a standing ovation at all three of them, and the press began openly speculating not if but when the unrepentantly chain-smoking Prime Minister, Charles Fortescue, would make way for the younger man. It started in the more sensational dailies, but in early September it was taken up by *The Times* in a leading article that was strongly rumoured to have been written by the editor himself. It was high time, suggested the article, for the Prime Minister to take his earldom and retire to his Worcestershire acres with good grace.

Charles Fortescue immediately announced that he intended to lead his party into the next general election, and this decision was publicly endorsed by the entire Cabinet, *with Rupert Massingham at the fore*. Such a demonstration of selfless loyalty, added to all his other qualities, made Rupert's position as heir apparent virtually unassailable. If and when, that is, the time ever came.

A damp and overcast summer had given way to a clear bright autumn. The Yardley Hunt's cubhunting season started on Thursday, 18 September. And owing to a more than usually congested legislative programme the House of Lords was due to resume after the Recess on Monday, 6 October, two weeks and a day before their colleagues in Another Place.

But it was on the morning of Thursday, 2 October that I received the telephone call.

'Hello, Derek? Jimmy McKay here. You remember I told you I'd get in touch if I ever heard anything about Rupert Massingham?'

'Yes.'

'Well, there may be something in this or there may not. You've seen that Charlie-boy's paying this surprise visit to Halverton, Rupert's constituency, tomorrow? The word is it's to demonstrate party unity, show their total confidence in one another, that sort of thing, but there's a smell about it that doesn't seem quite right somehow. It's the journalists they've invited, for one thing: not only key members of the Lobby – and that's highly unusual for occasions of this sort – but also the more scurrilous gossip-writers as well, Hector Waynefleet and his lot. That's all, but I thought it might be of interest to you.'

'Thanks, Jimmy,' I said.

Camberley's telephone number seemed to be constantly engaged, and I was some time getting through to her. She sounded surprised.

'Is this my call to you or yours to me?'

'Mine to you.'

'I've been trying to get through to you for ages, too. You start.'

I told her what Jimmy had said to me over the telephone. There was a brief pause.

'Yes, well, we've had our informant on again, and he says he knows for a fact the coup's going to start there tomorrow.'

'Look,' I said, 'the luncheon that Charles Fortescue's going to is to celebrate the hundredth anniversary of the Halverton Constitutional Club. I know the agent there very well, and I think I may be able to get us both in, if that would be any help.'

'That would be splendid. We'll drive up there together, shall we?'

I hesitated. It was at least worth a try.

'Could we have dinner together tonight? So that we can work out tactics for tomorrow,' I added lamely.

There was a distinct pause at Camberley's end of the line.

Then 'Not if it's *only* my intellect you're after. I do sometimes like to be looked on as a sex object, too,' she said.

We dined at Annabel's.

It was the first time that I had seen her for three weeks, and she was looking superb in a full-length dress of dark blue velvet, hitched up on one side and based loosely on a riding-habit, with a pair of gold boots with gilt spurs with rowels on them peeping out from beneath it. The whole thing was held together by a wrap-around belt of the same stuff, tied at the waist, and it only diverted, marginally, from the general theme at the neckline where it plunged with a kamikaze-like recklessness. One was left to imagine the stock.

When we danced, I discovered that she was one of those rare partners who are able to make even someone as inexpert as myself *know* that he is performing magnificently, and, even at a distance of three or four feet she contrived to render our shared movements an intimate sexual act.

166

I was thus confronted with a dilemma. Should I prolong the evening there for fear that, in spite of what she had said on the telephone, that might be the end of it? Or would there indeed be further and better things to come after it which it would be a pity to put off for too long?

I decided to err, if err it might turn out to be, on the side of optimism. We arrived back at her Wandsworth flat on the right side of midnight.

She didn't actually ask me in, but neither did she say anything when I followed her into the building and up the stairs. I waited while she manipulated her latch-key, until she had opened the door and held it open for me with one hand behind her as she felt for the light-switch with the other. It wasn't until we were in the sitting-room beyond that she turned and stood there smiling at me.

'Drink?' She nodded towards a full and varied tray of bottles on a side-table. 'Or . . . ?'

She put both thumbs under her belt, pulling it undone with one quick movement, gave a practised double flick of the head and an almost simultaneous shrug of her shoulders, so that the hair on either side arranged itself behind them, as the whole dress subsided gently to the floor. It was only then that I realised she hadn't been wearing anything underneath it at all.

True loveliness takes many different forms in accordance with the perception of the beholder but, there at that moment standing naked before me, Camberley Roberts was the most beautiful, the most desirable woman in the whole world.

I stood there transfixed – just looking at her. Silken russet locks caught in the glow of the lamp-light; prominent cheeks which emphasised the way that the corners of her violet eyes were crinkling at me; lips apart slightly to reveal beads of glistening teeth with the tip of a pink tongue protruding questingly out from between them; the creamy white tinged with pink of satin-smooth shoulders, dusted with tiny freckles and calling out for stroking where the slim arms hung beside her; the firm mounds of her breasts, their aureolas – apricot-coloured and having an almost translucent quality to them – moulded into a mouth-watering consistency; the gentle curve of a barely perceptible belly with its indent of a navel peeping shyly upwards from it; the little tufted foxy bit below, at the point where her thighs parted and long legs tapered deliciously downwards into the just higher than ankle-length golden-spurred boots, a puddle of fallen dark-blue velvet slopping around them on the floor.

Then I retraced my gaze and, slowly, luxuriously, savouringly, followed the whole sequence up again.

'Well,' the smile switched into that grin of hers, 'what are you waiting for?'

'I'll come quietly, Officer,' I said.

X

'WARE HARE

Friday, 3 October

I was watching Camberley, the slipstream through the open window ruffling stray tendrils of hair about her face, as she drove my Citroën up the motorway with far greater precision than I myself could have done. Suddenly I realised that I wasn't going to be satisfied any longer with the sporadic meetings that had been all that she had been able to spare for me over the past few weeks.

'Er. . . . '

She glanced at me sideways, the grin hovering in the wings.

'No!' she said.

'You haven't heard the question yet.'

'Will I shack up with you? Or did you have something a bit more permanent in mind? The answer's still "no".'

'Why not?'

'Last night was something special. It was . . . oh, I don't know, a sort of dream somehow . . . a one–off, and it'd be a pity to spoil it. I'd like to be able to remember it just the way it was.'

'That's nonsense,' I said, 'and you know it. There'll be other times – not quite the same, perhaps, but just as good.'

'Well . . . perhaps. But there are other reasons, too.'

'Such as?'

'I like my job too much, for one thing, and I don't want to have to give it up. Not yet anyway. You need somebody who can be a wife to you, bear your children, be a hostess for your political career.'

'That doesn't matter,' I said. But, even as I said it, I knew that it did – and I wasn't quite sure how much. 'You said *reason. .s*. Give me another.'

'At the *moment critique* last night – well, one of the *moments* – you called me "Julia". You're still in love with her. You may not know it but you are. And I'm damned if I'm going to spend the rest of my life being a surrogate,' she said.

I sat back and enjoyed the unaccustomed luxury of being able to look about me, which gave the passing scenery on either side a new and panoramic dimension. The outline of a castellated folly – or was it perhaps a genuine ruin; the medley of autumn reds, yellows and browns on tree and hedgerow of the undulating and surprisingly rural Hertfordshire landscape; the little village away to the left of us, church spire set on a hilltop with cottages clustered around it in a Christmas-card formation. Things that, in all the years that I had been driving myself along this stretch of motorway, I had only been able to see out of the corner of my eye.

Looking back on it long after the whole thing was over, I wondered why such a seemingly final rejection by Camberley shouldn't have wrecked the whole day for me – which somehow it didn't. Perhaps it was just that I hadn't been prepared to accept the fact that she really meant it. Or perhaps I had had a subconscious awareness that there might possibly be something in what she said about myself and Julia.

And then I did realise why.

All the time, with another part of my mind, I had been acquiring the steadily growing conviction that, unlikely though it might seem, something really was going to happen that day at Halverton. The whole drive had progressively been taking on that sense of uncertainty and anticipation that goes to make up the excitement of a hunting morning. The sun was shining from behind us, but there was a frost in the air that hadn't been there earlier and a bit of a breeze but not too much – near-perfect conditions for a scent.

It was thus that Camberley and I sat in silence until we reached the start of the three-mile stretch of contraflow system that traversed the exit which led to the southern part of Rupert's constituency as well as to my own village of Thyrde.

Roadworks seemed to have become endemic on the sixty-odd miles of my route to and from London – as soon as one batch was finished another sprang up a mile or two away – and queues forming where three lanes were condensed into two had for some time been lengthening the journey considerably. Here, however, the position seemed to have eased somewhat. It was still only 11.30 in the morning, and the Friday rush-hour traffic would not start building up until an hour or two later. Only the fast southbound lane was now on our carriageway in contraflow, the slow one on the other side now being in operation, which left us, including the hard shoulder, with still three lanes going north. Furthermore, when we reached the junction itself, the entrances and exits on both sides were open, which was a definite bonus over what had been before.

'Straight ahead here,' I said to Camberley. 'It's quicker to go off at the next one for Halverton.'

The old market-town had been considerably enlarged in recent years and, until the boundary changes prior to the last General Election, had together with its Constitutional Club formed the focal point of the far larger constituency of Halverton which had also embraced the more rural area in which Thyrde was situated. I had been president of its Conservative Association. Both the agent, Jack Ferris, who was an old friend of mine, and the chairman had opted to stay with the newly compact constituency, formed of the town itself and the immediately surrounding countryside and keeping the old name; the outgoing Member had taken over its presidency, while I had been made president of the offshoot with its completely new set-up next door.

As we drove into the outskirts of the town and I became aware of the groups of policemen standing at almost every corner which proliferated as we approached the centre, my sense of apprehension quickened.

'Do you think they could have got wind of something, too?' I said.

But Camberley shook her head.

'No, this is standard form anywhere the Prime Minister goes nowadays. Even so, they've done well with such short notice. We've alerted his own detectives to be on extra guard of course.'

'And how did they react?'

'With remarkably little interest. Said they have to be prepared for anything at any time. I have been given the name of a local man to contact, though.'

'And what will be he able to do?'

'Play it by ear. Same as us,' she said.

The one-way system around the town centre of Halverton has always struck me as having been designed by a maker of Chinese puzzles. Whenever you're trying to get in from outside the streets always seem to be running the wrong way and exactly the same applies when you're trying to get out again. But Camberley and I had left ourselves plenty of time and, after a number of false starts, we eventually saw the little market-square with the peculiar front elevation of the late-Victorian building at the far side of it straight ahead.

Consisting of three storeys as well as a basement, the Halverton Constitutional Club had been designed by one of the foremost architects of the period, but I doubt if even the late Sir John Betjeman would have been able to work up a great deal of enthusiasm over its preservation. Its foremost feature on the drawing-board had been an intricate wrought-iron balcony running its full width at first-floor level, from which it was intended that Tory candidates successful in the polls should address their electors gathered after the declaration in the square below. And, if this design had been carried out, all would have been well.

The sitting Member of the time, Sir William Hollowell, had come to the conclusion that he would be seen to better effect if the balcony were to be transferred to the second- or top-floor level and, as he personally was to pay for the greater part of the building costs, his wishes were respected. The architect promptly resigned in disgust and would have nothing further to do with the construction. The finished result had a curiously top-heavy aspect of the kind that one associates with a far older building and which I personally, having known it from my childhood, had always found rather endearing. It had also had the effect, until the advent of modern means of mass communication, of making the occupant of the balcony virtually inaudible to the crowds below – but perhaps in Sir William's case this had been just as well.

We parked the Citroën in the slot that Jack Ferris had reserved for me in the carpark at the back, next but one to a blood-red Rover which I rightly assumed to be Rupert's official car, and I led Camberley round the side of the building and in at the massive entrance up a flight of steps at the front.

The room on the left was thronged and smoke-filled, most of the visible faces vaguely familiar to me. One party, hunting farmers from that part of the Yardley country that was in Rupert's constituency who were noisily ordering drinks at the bar, beckoned us over.

Camberley paused in her stride. 'I'm in your hands. Do we join them?'

I thought quickly.

'No. If anything's going to happen at this stage, it'll be on the top floor where the nobs are,' I said, hoping to God that I was right.

I made apologetic gestures to my friends and led her up the stairs, past the main function room on the first floor, where luncheon was laid and which ought to have had french windows and the balcony to lead out onto, and on up to the rather less imposing room on the second, which actually did.

This was a narrow dingy room devoid of any form of decoration, and, as was usual with him, the small number of people that it contained were gathered round Rupert Massingham at the far end. I searched anxiously amongst them to see if Julia was there, but luckily she wasn't. Whatever was going to happen, I was glad that she wouldn't be part of it and, even though I was by now reconciled to the prospect of seeing her with Rupert, I somehow felt that it might be embarrassing when I had Camberley beside me.

It did occur to me then that it should by rights have been even more embarrassing for *him*.

Jack Ferris, with an expression of total concentration on his face, was engaged in laying a trail of metal ashtrays on every conceivable surface that was likely to be on the Prime Minister's route and, as he put one down by the doorway where we were standing, I tapped him on the shoulder and introduced him to Camberley.

'Thank you so much for getting us in,' I said.

'That's all right, Derek. You know everybody, I think. Get yourselves a drink, will you? I must go down and prepare for the PM's arrival.' And he bustled off again, a little clutch of the remaining ashtrays in his hand.

I got hold of a couple of glasses of gin and tonic as protective colouring for each of us. Then I started to search the room to see if there was anything or anybody that might give the slightest cause for suspicion, pointing out the assembled company to Camberley as I did so.

'The tall thin chap is Lord Halverton, Rupert's predecessor and my opposite number as president of the Association. That's his wife beside him, and the small girl with the Alice-band and hair to match is their daughter, Penelope. Her doting parents call her "Penny-Sweet".'

'Yuk!' said Camberley.

'She is a bit yukky, but I suppose it's not her fault, poor little beast. The fellow on Rupert's other side is the Euro-MP, covers this Westminster constituency as well as the one I live in and half a dozen others. That's the chairman he's talking to, and the Mayor of Halverton's with them in his chain of office, he's a Labour man but liked by all parties equally.'

I peered over beyond them. 'There is someone I don't know, though.'

'The bald jolly-faced man?'

'That's him.'

'I rather think that he may be my police contact,' Camberley said.

At that moment Rupert happened to glance in our direction, noticed our presence for the first time and, leaving his companions gaping, strode over towards us with the aspect of a power-drill. It was the first time that

I had seen him since the puppy show, and no doubt the incident there, and more particularly the fact of my having witnessed it, still rankled.

'What do you think you're doing here, Derek?' He ignored Camberley who, after her initial surprise, seemed amused rather than put out by it.

'Perhaps you'd like to see our invitations?' I said. 'By the way, you do remember Camberley Roberts?'

'Eh? Oh, sorry, m'dear.' And he gave her a desultory kiss on the cheek. Then he glared at me again. 'I'll talk to *you* later,' he said and went back to the party he had been with.

I looked at my watch. The Prime Minister was well overdue now, and I had a sudden moment of panic. Could he already have been got at by an accomplice on the way here – actually coming into the Constitutional Club, perhaps – leaving Rupert with the perfect alibi two floors above? Wouldn't we have done better at least to have awaited his arrival downstairs with my friends in the bar?

I leant towards Camberley, but before I had time to say anything Charles Fortescue himself came through the door accompanied by wreaths of cigarette smoke, Michael Percy his Parliamentary Private Secretary and a couple of detectives, the whole party shepherded by Jack Ferris. Instead of passing on down the room to where Rupert was waiting to receive him, he stopped by us, thereby earning me another look of fury from our mutual host.

'Hello, Derek. I didn't know you were from these parts.' He looked pointedly at Camberley.

'Good morning, Prime Minister. Yes, I'm from the next-door constituency. Can I introduce Camberley Roberts?'

'How do you do? You're one of Rupert Massingham's constituents, are you? Lucky feller.'

'No, I'm just a friend of Derek's, I'm afraid.'

'Ah, well, it's he who's the lucky one, then.' He put his half-finished cigarette down on the nearest of Jack's ashtrays, took a gold case out of his pocket, held it out to Camberley and when she refused lit another for himself.

'He looks well enough,' I said in an undertone to Michael Percy, who was fidgeting about beside me in the vain hope of persuading his principal to move on.

'Always does. He's had one hell of a week, though, and meetings all day tomorrow and Sunday at Chequers as well. We're driving straight on there this afternoon.'

'How's it going generally?'

'So-so.' The PPS held out his hand palm downwards, tilting it one way and then the other, balance-fashion. 'If only we could stop the PM chain-smoking, in public at any rate – that's the thing that seems to infuriate people most. There's still plenty of our supporters who won't be satisfied until Rupert takes over, in spite of that generous renunciation act of his.'

I myself wasn't so sure. I looked at the Prime Minister obviously revelling in his conversation with Camberley, red weather-beaten face, grizzled moustache, right hand with gently smoke-wreathing cigarette between the fingers held out in that pose made famous by every cartoonist in the country, and marvelled once again at the sense of presence that he emitted so effortlessly. I reckoned that, even for Rupert and even in his present ascendancy, in the normal course of events Charles Fortescue would be a hard man to replace.

I became aware of Penny-Sweet, who had been standing unnoticed just to one side of him, looking upwards with a particularly seraphic expression on her face and holding a buttonhole, red carnation backed with asparagus fern, by its silver-paper wrapped stalk.

She gave a little tug to his sleeve, and he turned.

'For me? Bless you, my dear.' And Camberley caught my eye, totally expressionless, as he bent to kiss Penny-Sweet's little uptilted face.

Then he straightened up again. 'Ah, well, see you later, Derek. I promised to run through my speech notes with Rupert before luncheon.' He gave a parting pat to Penny-Sweet's golden hair and, Michael fussing after him, strolled away, taking out of his inside breast-pocket as he did so a folded wad of A4 paper sheets.

'I think I'll just go and make my name with my police contact. Won't be a moment,' Camberley said.

Left alone, I wandered over to the french windows and looked out on to the famous Hollowell balcony. It was from here that Charles Fortescue and Rupert would be making an appearance to the crowds in the square below after luncheon. And then another thought struck me. Could this be where and when it would happen, a quick heave over the flimsy-looking wrought-iron balustrade, a rifle aimed from a neighbouring rooftop perhaps, either way the spread-eagled body and the long fall downwards?

This was ridiculous. I was getting paranoid. We were in England, and things like that just didn't happen here.

Did they?

I stood on tip-toe and peered over the precarious balcony, immediately wishing that I hadn't. I stepped quickly backwards. It couldn't have been much over forty feet to the ground below, but it certainly seemed more and I never did have a head for heights.

I looked across at Rupert and Charles Fortescue, heads bent together over the unfolded sheaf of notes, and the others in their various groupings and regroupings, and it was then that I had a merciful distraction. There among them, talking to her bald jolly-faced man as though they were old friends newly discovered after a long period of having lost touch with one another, stood Camberley –

178

demure in the simple square-necked grey woollen dress that she was wearing. I thought of that glorious body of hers beneath it. Did she really mean it that I wasn't to be allowed access to its joys, ever again?

Suddenly this seemed to put all my feverish imaginings back into their proper perspective again. The Prime Minister's two detectives were there, as was Rupert's own, and I myself had seen the hoards of policemen gathered at every vantage-point outside the building, so how *could* anything happen? Surely the whole thing would turn out to be nothing more than it purported to be, an open declaration of solidarity between two prominent statesmen, a political occasion ordinary to the point of dullness, after all.

My instant feeling of relief was curiously followed by one of flatness and even disappointment.

It was only then that I noticed the newcomer, standing slightly apart from the others, whose face seemed vaguely familiar. Hair slicked back, neat blue pin-stripe suit, dark blue tie with the Conservative torch logo on it. No, it couldn't be, here in these surroundings.

'And yet . . . ?

Ralph. His rat-like acne-studded face was one that I had been sure I would never forget. This boy certainly wasn't wearing ear-rings, but he was standing too far away for me to see if his left ear had holes pierced in it where they might have been. I looked quickly away again to avoid any risk of catching his eye, because he would certainly know by now that I was here if it was indeed he, but it might at least be helpful if I could manage to keep him in ignorance of the fact that I had recognised him.

'Hello. It's me. I'm back.'

I looked round to find that Camberley had rejoined me.

'Listen,' I said.

But at that moment there was a stirring among the occupants of the room, and Rupert and the Prime Minister made for the door. We followed on behind them and, as we did so, I just had time to alert her in a whisper to the possibility of a much transformed Ralph being present. I noticed Charles Fortescue lighting yet another cigarette at the top of the stairs ahead of me – he had only just disposed of his previous one – and three-quarters of the way down he had to lay that, too, aside; there was a window-seat upholstered in red plastic running the length of a half-landing, and the last in line of Jack Ferris's trail of metal ashtrays was strategically placed in the exact centre of that.

The principal room of the Halverton Constitutional Club, high-ceilinged, high-windowed and occupying the whole frontage of the first floor, had deteriorated sadly since its opening exactly one hundred years ago that day. The surface of the walls under their faded mid-blue paint was patched and uneven in some places and cracked in others with white streaks showing through. Even the regularly spaced plaster motifs, harps and crossed trumpets enwreathed in laurel leaves, that had once been their proudest feature, had been coarsened and misshapen, successive layerings of more economical gold paint having done duty for the original gold leaf.

One long table with named places, as yet unfilled, ran the length of the room with its back to the doorway through which we came in. The bulk of the company, my friends from the bar downstairs amongst them, were already seated round the sprigs that branched out from it in the direction of the windows. They stood up and clapped as the top-table party filed in.

I had been warned by Jack Ferris in advance that we would have to find seats where we could in the body of the room, so I hurried Camberley round to a couple of empty ones that I spotted at the top of one of the sprigs nearest to the Prime Minister, narrowly beating his PPS, Michael

Percy, and his two detectives to them. All three hovered for a moment giving us meaningful looks, but we stood firm – just at that moment we had a far greater claim than they did – and they had to go off and find themselves places further away at the window end. A clergyman, presumably the local parson who had materialised from somewhere, said grace, the whole party sat down again noisily and luncheon began.

I was totally unaware of what we were eating, but I reckon that from previous experience of such functions I could give a reasonably accurate summary: one of those indeterminate soups that come under the generic heading of 'Brown Windsor' followed by pre-carved and reheated slices of overdone roast beef, lathered with tepid gravy and accompanied by under-roast potatoes and soggy individual discs of Yorkshire pudding, and then either fruit salad out of a tin or a just passable apple-pie.

I myself was too much on edge even to make an attempt at smalltalk, and I envied Camberley her imperturbability as she struck up a conversation about show jumping with her neighbour on the other side. I knew instinctively that she was at the same time keeping herself aware of everything that was going on around us – probably with an even greater alertness than I.

Rupert was occupying the centre of the top table with the Mayor on his left and the Prime Minister on his right, then came Lord Halverton and Penny-Sweet with the Chairman, poor chap, on her other side. At one of the nearby sprigs, I saw Jimmy McKay sitting with a group consisting of a number of Lobby journalists whom I recognised together with three or four supercilious-looking young men whom I didn't – these presumably being the gossip columnists but, as they all looked very much the same, I was unable to identify the dreaded Hector Waynefleet amongst them. Jimmy was holding an untouched glass of white wine out in front of him and he looked down at it with an expression of helpless horror which was only half-feigned as I caught his eye.

The loyal toast had been proposed immediately after the first course, in order no doubt to enable the principal guest to resume smoking at the earliest-possible moment, and as soon as the coffee had been handed round and the waitresses left the room Rupert rose to his feet.

'Mr Mayor, Prime Minister, my lords, ladies and gentle-men. . . . '

Without any prior notice having been given, the whole room had instantly fallen silent, and every other person there seemed to be held in an electric atmosphere from which only I was immune. What he was saying seemed to me to be ordinary enough, although I only heard the actual words with part of my attention. The qualities and prestige of Charles Fortescue and the honour that he was today doing to Halverton, the history of the Constitutional Club itself and, by implication, the honour that Halverton was today doing to him, the fact that since its opening he was the seventh Conservative prime minister to have lunched or dined in that hall.

Then I caught sight of the boy Ralph, where he was sitting furthest across the room from me. I kept my eyes on him and, at one moment, I saw him looking intently at Rupert. I glanced at the latter and managed to intercept the slightest of nods that he gave in mid-speech, then back at Ralph again, who got up, murmured something to the people on either side of him and made his way round the tables towards the doorway. I gave a totally superfluous nudge to Camberley's elbow, and we both watched as he passed by a few yards away from us and slipped out of the room.

'That's him. I'm sure of it,' I whispered, although the left side of his head had been away from me and I still hadn't been able to see the holes where the twin ear-rings might have been.

Almost at the same moment I saw one of the waitresses approaching Michael Percy where he was sitting, his eyes fixed on Charles Fortescue like those of a well-trained gundog on his master, tap him on the shoulder to gain his attention and pass a note to him. He glanced at it and shook his head impatiently. But she leant over to murmur something in his ear and, casting one more slightly worried look in the direction of the Prime Minister, he too got up and followed her round the tables and out of the door.

I now knew with an awful sense of inevitability that whatever it was that Camberley and I had come all this way to Halverton for *was* going to happen, that Rupert himself would be responsible for it, that he had planned the whole event with this one purpose in mind. It was no longer a question of whether but of precisely when. And we were sitting there powerless to prevent it. We still hadn't got the slightest idea as to what it was going to be, so what was there to prevent?

It had become as though a play were being acted out in front of us in dumb show for our own especial benefit. *Charles Fortescue slowly and deliberately putting his latest cigarette out and leaving it among the other stubs already in the ashtray in front of him. Giving a gentle tap to his coat at the point where it covered the inside breast-pocket in which he had kept his speech notes. A sudden look of concern, feeling in that pocket and then successively in all his others. Peering helplessly towards the empty space where his PPS had been sitting. Rupert Massingham resuming his seat amidst applause from the whole room, which died slowly away as the general gaze was turned expectantly in the direction of the Prime Minister himself.*

Charles Fortescue whispering to Rupert in the sudden silence, again tapping his pocket. Rupert pointing towards the ceiling with a look of enquiry on his face. Lord Halverton leaning over solicitously. Another whispered conversation. Charles Fortescue making to get to his feet. Lord Halverton putting a firm hand on his shoulder and turning to Penny-Sweet, this time he pointing towards the ceiling. Penny-Sweet nodding excitedly, jumping to her feet, giving a hop and a skip and a twirl, her arms outstretched, a little bow to the room at large, turning and trotting out through the door.

Myself sitting there transfixed as conversation broke out again in a desultory fashion around the tables, gained momentum and finally became general.

Then, gradually, I became aware of another sensation. That somewhat acrid smell . . . could it be burning . . . the pace quickened . . . smoke was coming through the door now . . . there was a sudden raucous clatter of bells outside . . . the whole room was on its feet . . . the noise transforming itself into a hubbub . . . Rupert putting his hand on Charles Fortescue's shoulder . . .

'This way, Prime Minister.'

The spell was shattered. . . .

I had to do something. Anything. Create a diversion.

But what?

'Rupert!' I shouted.

And I lunged across the table between us and grabbed his arm.

He turned and faced me, hesitating. The human part of the cacophony stopped instantly, and for a moment every movement in the room froze into a tableau.

Then 'Oh my God,' said Charles Fortescue, 'that poor little girl,' and he turned and ran through the open doorway into the smoke and up the stairs.

I had totally forgotten about Penny-Sweet and so, from their stunned reaction, had all the others. Placed where I was, I couldn't have followed him even if I'd been capable of movement just at that moment. But there was only the briefest of pauses before one of his detectives elbowed his way through the standing throng and raced up after him.

After that, it all happened very quickly. There was a stamping on the landing outside and yellow-helmeted firemen, wearing the grotesque masks of breathing apparatus, were visible through the open doorway, some already turning hoses on the burning half-landing.

'This way, ladies and gentlemen, please,' said another of the firemen, this one with a white helmet. 'Quietly does it. There's no cause for alarm,' and, under his watchful eye, the Chairman guided a dazed Lord Halverton and a protesting Rupert over towards a second door that I hadn't noticed before, at the far end of the room.

I took Camberley by the elbow and, with remarkable lack of fuss, everybody filed quietly after them and, following the directions of the fireman, down a back staircase, through a side-door and out into the welcome relief of clean fresh October air.

Round the corner of the building, the sunlit square was thronged with people all gazing upwards in an atmosphere of breathless suspense, but two fire-engines had somehow managed to negotiate their way through them, one a water-tender and the other fitted with a turntable ladder. There was utter silence as this latter, a diminutive yellow-helmeted figure already perched precariously on the little platform at the top of it, swung itself slowly round on its gantry so as to point in the right direction; extended its component lengths until it had achieved the precise height that it needed; and, finally, dipped its head just low enough to establish contact with that ornate second-floor balcony, where Her Majesty's Prime Minister and First Lord of the Treasury, his detective beside him, stood waiting patiently as he murmured words of comfort to the cowering form of Penny-Sweet clasped in his arms.

A second fireman had already started scuttling up the ladder, as the one at the top clambered over the wrought-iron railing. He took the little girl from Charles Fortescue, waited for his colleague to reach them and passed her gently over. Then, after watching them start safely on their downward journey, he and the detective together helped the Prime Minister over and on to the rungs of the ladder.

Still there was silence. But, as they, too, made their way downwards, starting as no more than a murmur on the outskirts, spreading through the crowd and gathering force as it did so, there rose to a crescendo such a volume of cheering as exceeded anything that the little market-square of Halverton could have dreamt of and, if only for this one time in the Constitutional Club's entire history, justified every penny that the Constitutional Club's eccentric founder, Sir William Hollowell, had spent.

'Look out, he's getting away,' I said to Camberley.

Compulsively, we had stood and watched as they reached the bottom of the ladder – and thereafter. Penny-Sweet being handed into the arms of her father; Rupert Massingham being the first to congratulate the Prime Minister and then discreetly making way for a succession of others; a tearful Lord Halverton gripping Charles Fortescue's hand, and the Press surging round with their cameras; Michael Percy forcing his way through to him and, eventually, the detectives together with local policemen clearing a path for them through crowds reluctant to allow them away.

It was only as we turned away that I had caught sight of the blood-red shape of Rupert's official Rover nosing off the wrong way down a one-way street.

Suddenly, without my having noticed anything that could have been a prearranged signal pass between them, the bald-headed man was at Camberley's side. 'Sorry, Derek, I'll have to go with the Inspector now,' she leant over and kissed me on the cheek, 'but follow us if you like,' she added. And, without anything further by way of explanation or apology, the two of them hurried over to a police car that was parked across the street from me, drove off with lights flashing and siren sounding and were gone.

My immediate reaction was one of utter mortification at the unfairness of it all: to think that after all these months I should be left behind, abandoned by Camberley, just at the very moment when the whole thing seemed to be coming to fruition. And then I had to concede that once it had become official she probably had no alternative and, at least, those last words of hers had meant that I wasn't to be entirely excluded. Either way, I was doing no good to myself or anyone else by standing there moping and I ran off round the corner of the Constitutional Club building in the direction of the carpark, to collect my Citroën from where I had left it at the back.

Then I stopped dead.

The boy Ralph was coming out of a side-door of the club, carrying in both hands something that was loosely wrapped up in newspaper.

Now really was the time for instant decision. Should I carry on with my original plan of trying to drive after the others in their pursuit of Rupert with the all too likely risk of missing the way that they had gone? Or would it perhaps be wiser to stay with Ralph and either confront him here or follow him wherever he might be going in the hope that at least whatever it was that he was carrying so carefully might prove to be incriminating?

But, at that moment, the question was answered for me.

Rupert's official Rover must have contained only his detective and his driver. Camberley and her contact had gone off on a false scent which had without doubt been carefully laid for anyone who might be suspicious enough to want to follow it. It was too late to get them back now, and I really was on my own.

Because the car that approached from round the bend in the road to the front of me, slewed across to my side and came to a momentary halt in order to take in Ralph and his burden through its offside rear door, did a quick U-turn and shot off again to disappear in the same direction as that from which it had come was unmistakably the silver BMW, DWK 49 T, and equally unmistakably Rupert Massingham was at its wheel.

XI

FULL CRY

Friday, 3 October (continued)

I ran just as fast as I could round to the carpark at the back, jumped into my own car and drove off in the direction that Rupert and Ralph had taken. I was pretty sure that neither of them had spotted me, so it was hardly likely that they would be taking any conscious action to evade pursuers. Even so, it was vital that I should be able to catch up with them before, in the normal course of events, they took any turning off to the right or to the left.

One thing was clear: both Camberley's tip-off and Jimmy McKay's instinct had now been shown to be justified. A deliberate attempt to kill, or at least severely injure, the Prime Minister had only just been averted. The events of the afternoon, coming after such warnings from two separate and distinct sources, would surely have been far too great a coincidence if something along those lines hadn't been intended right from the start.

The Prime Minister had been careless enough to leave behind in the room upstairs the notes for the vitally important speech that he had been rehearsing so carefully with Rupert; and this, for a start, must have been skilfully stage-managed. Just exactly how Rupert had intended to lure Charles Fortescue himself up into the fire that had been deliberately started for that purpose – even if Penny-Sweet hadn't gone tripping off after them, it seemed inconceivable that someone, his PPS perhaps or one of his detectives, wouldn't have gone for him – and how my clumsy attempt at an intervention had had the effect of short-circuiting the planned sequence of events remained a mystery. But that both of these initial hypotheses were correct I now had no doubt at all.

I was beginning to think that I was too late and that I never would succeed in catching up with the BMW when, coming in sight of a T-junction at the far end of the street, I was just in time to see its tail end disappearing round the corner to the right.

I was now faced with an entirely new problem and one that simply hadn't occurred to me before. Should I try to stop the car in front of me and confront its occupants? There were two of them to my one, and the tuition that Camberley had give me had been defensive rather than *off*ensive and, even if I were successful, what on earth did I do then?

Clearly I needed a witness to confirm that Ralph, who might or might not have a police record and who might or might not have in his possession something that was incriminating, was being driven away from the near-disaster at the Halverton Constitutional Club by Rupert Massingham. But I remembered all too vividly the total failure that I had had in convincing my political superiors even when I was using channels that were by custom open to me. Could I really imagine myself going up to a local country police-man and saying, 'Excuse me, Officer, but that's the Home Secretary in front and I think you ought to arrest him because I happen to know that he's just tried to murder the Prime Minister' – and, if I were to do so, just what sort of a reception could I expect to get?

I was still pondering over this problem as we came out of the maze that was central Halverton, and the best that I had been able to come up with was this. That I should continue to follow the BMW taking care not to get close enough to be recognised by either of its occupants and thereby lose the only advantage that I reckoned that I had so far. And that I should trust to some sort of inspiration turning up when the moment, whatever that might be, came.

We followed a tortuous route along roads none of which I recognised until I found that we had come out on to the mile or so of dual carriageway that led back to the Halverton junction of the M1. It was only as I was actually passing it that I saw out of the corner of my eye the blood-red Rover in a layby at the side, with the white police car drawn up in front of it. Camberley and her contact were the very reinforcements that I needed, and my foot was immediately poised over the brake pedal. The risk of losing contact altogether with Rupert and Ralph was only a slight one, because it was a fair bet that they were on their way back to London now.

But at that actual moment the BMW put on a sudden spurt, Rupert too having obviously seen the juxtaposition of the police car with his own decoy, and I had to make an instant decision. I came to the conclusion that I just didn't dare to risk it and, blaring on my horn in the hope of attracting Camberley's attention, I transferred my foot to the accelerator and set off again in fast pursuit.

I was gaining on the car in front when, sure enough, it disappeared down the slip-road that led to the southbound carriageway. It was only after I, too, had turned that I found out how badly I had misjudged the distance. As the BMW filtered on to the motorway, my Citroën following, I could make out through the glass of the rear window in front of me the white blob of Ralph's face staring back.

The need for caution was over, that was one consolation. But with the occupants now aware of the fact that I was behind them it was absolutely imperative that I shouldn't

191

lose touch with the car in front of me whatever it might proceed to do. The luxury of being able to look about me on the motorway was also a thing of the past.

Rupert's first tactic was simply to try to outrun me. It was clear from the beginning that he was the better driver, but the BMW was certainly no faster than my Citroën and I just managed to keep up with it. If I could only hold on until the point where three lanes converged into two in preparation for the contraflow system that traversed the next junction, I ought to be able to rely on obtaining at least a certain amount of respite then.

I had fully expected to find a queue of slow-moving and stationary cars at that point, but it was still too early in the day and, when we reached it, although the traffic did slow down, there was no actual wait. Even so, we weren't able to do more than about fifty and we cruised along at this speed, I following Rupert, both of us in the faster of the two lanes. But just as we were approaching the point where the two diverged Rupert suddenly pulled over to the left-hand lane, braked and drew back, keeping his car level with mine in such a way that it made it totally impossible for me to do the same.

I received a momentary impression of Ralph's grinning face, nose pressed against the window as he waved derisively to me with the fingers of both his hands. And as my own stream of traffic carried me relentlessly off, over and on to the other carriageway, I saw the BMW leaving the motorway at that junction by the exit road.

With Rupert now off the motorway and I still on it, the only thing that I could do was to get off it myself as quickly as possible, which meant at the next junction. I drove on as fast as the traffic in my contraflow lane would let me. Meanwhile, I had only as long as this might take to make up my mind about the next question, which was: just exactly what did I do then?

Assuming that Rupert was still intending to go back to London, he could now be making for the A5 or he could be cutting across country in the other direction to the A1, but there had also been a third option open to him.

The junction at which he had so skilfully contrived that he and I should part company also happened to be the one that I regularly used myself, and during the time that this had been closed altogether, unable to turn left at the roundabout on to the motorway, I had had to go straight over, then on for a mile or two and take a little minor road also to the left. This meandered in a leisurely fashion back towards the motorway, crossed it by a bridge, went through a small village and eventually connected up with a main road coming from the east just before the point where it, too, joined the motorway at the junction for which I was now making. Rupert, coming to London from his house in his constituency, would also have had to use this diversion, though it would probably never have occurred to him that I coming from Thyrde would know about it too and I was pretty sure in my own mind that this was the route that he would have decided to take.

As soon as I too was off the motorway, I turned the car in the main road and stopped facing the point where the little by-road joined it. Had I made the right decision? Even if I had, would Rupert have made use of the diversion to jettison his passenger?

But my confidence only dissipated marginally as I waited and, sure enough, after two or three minutes I saw the silver BMW come out on to the main road ahead of me, cross it and filter down the slip-road on to the motorway again. Ralph was still in it. His face, which I saw through the rear window as I followed and came up close behind them again, had lost its grin as well as every trace of derision now.

I was still no further forward as to what to do when and if I did manage to stop the BMW, but I was damned if I was going to lose them now. That Rupert was equally determined to get away from *me* soon became apparent, and from then on he went through every conceivable manoeuvre to achieve this effect.

First, he jammed his brakes on suddenly in the hope that I should run into his rear bumper, but I had been ready for that one as, luckily, had the motorist behind me. Next, he pulled into the slow lane, slowed down quickly until he was level with me just as he had before, but this time trying to ride me out on to the fast lane and into the path of an overtaking Bentley, using much the same technique as he had at the Yardley Hunt point-to-point. Then he signalled that he was turning off the motorway again at a junction, turned to the left only to swing back in again at the very last moment once he saw that I was safely following. Again, he waited for a fast car to be almost up with us, and darted out in front of it, I only just managing to do so too with impunity.

What were for Rupert finely calculated risks, when it came to my turn became near-suicidal, but I was only dimly conscious of this, caught up as I now was in all the excitement and sense of euphoria that went to make up the thrill of the chase.

I still hadn't got the slightest idea as to whether or not Camberley and her police friend were following. If only I'd got a telephone in my car, I thought, I could have made some sort of contact, and I made a mental note to have one installed at the earliest-possible moment. But one thing did occur to me, the very fact that Rupert was prepared to go to such lengths to lose me confirmed what I had only before suspected, that either whatever it was that Ralph had in his parcel – some form of incendiary device, I was pretty certain – or possibly even the presence of Ralph himself was, at least in Rupert's eyes, highly incriminating.

And, as so often happens, it was only when I had stopped actively thinking about the problem of what to do with the car in front of me that the answer suddenly came to me. I'd need to be off the motorway for a start – and we were nearing the end of it now – because there'd have to be a policeman handy when I stopped Rupert's car. The scenario as I visualised it would go something like this.

First, I would beckon over the policeman.

'That's Sir Rupert Massingham, the Home Secretary, Officer. Thank God I've caught up with you, Rupert. This man I saw you pick up and give a lift to in Northamptonshire, I'm pretty sure he's the same chap who tried to mug me with three of his friends, several months back in London.'

Then I would turn to the policeman again.

'If I *am* right, you'd better watch out for him, and he was looking very furtive over something he was carrying wrapped up in newspaper. That's it there.'

It was possible that Ralph might panic and try to make a run for it at this point, and I'd have to watch out for that. If he did, it would certainly be evidence of his guilt. If he didn't, however, Rupert would either have to admit that Ralph was known to him or confirm my suggestion that he had picked him up as a casual hitch-hiker in Halverton. In either event, he wouldn't be able to prevent my mugging charge being investigated, and Camberley would be a witness to this.

Taking it one step further, Camberley would also be able to testify not only to Ralph having been at the luncheon but also to his having left the room at the vital moment, and it might even be possible to establish the fact that Rupert himself had been responsible for his presence there in the first place.

It was with this plan of action firmly embedded in my mind, then, that I followed the BMW off the motorway and along the North Circular. Off the North Circular again and out on to Hendon Way. It only remained for me to await the right combination of conditions arising to enable me to put it into effect.

In practice, this wasn't anything like as easy as I'd thought it would be. Rupert proved to be particularly adept at threading his way through lines of unhurried home-going traffic, but my own determination to keep with him at whatever the cost managed to overcome that. Up Finchley Road to the Tower Garage at the top and then downhill again. The only trouble was that not only did every traffic-light seem to be with him but also every time I looked around for a policeman there wasn't a single one in sight.

Left into Arkwright Road, and there indeed was a policeman walking down the pavement towards us but there wasn't a chance of overtaking the BMW and stopping it at that point; the cars parked along both sides of the road precluded that.

Right again at the top and down Fitzjohn's Avenue, plenty of room to overtake but no policeman, no passerby even. Left at Swiss Cottage and into Adelaide Road. This, too, was a route that I had often used myself, but I wouldn't have expected Rupert to have been aware of that, either.

Right into King Henry's Road – *which King Henry and why did he have a road just there*? Down Primrose Hill, right into St Mark's Square, left into Albert Road and straight on and over. Was it my imagination, or did he seem to be tiring now? Still no policeman, still no red or amber light.

It was as we were approaching the point where he would have to cross over Euston Road into Gower Street, with the gaunt grey shape of the Post Office Tower looming menacingly ahead of us, that Rupert decided to have one last try. He deliberately hung back until the traffic-lights had turned to amber and, when the red followed, made as if to stop. Then he shot forward again at what ought by all the rules to have been the very last moment. I had no alternative but to go after him, by this time I couldn't have stopped myself even if I'd wanted to and how I escaped hitting something I still can't imagine. But I was safely over, carrying away with me no more than a fleeting impression of horns blaring and a raucous jamming on of brakes.

Down Gower Street, over Oxford Street and right into Shaftesbury Avenue, I was close on his heels now and we were coming into an area where policemen abounded. If all else failed, I thought, I could ram the BMW from behind and say my piece in the resulting confusion. The end must be in sight.

The end when it did come was all too simple, but it was none the less devastating for that.

At Cambridge Circus I had been unable to prevent a little black beetle Volkswagen from insinuating itself between my own Citroën and the BMW. Then, at Leicester Square Underground station, the lights must have been out of phase, because they turned green for just long enough to let Rupert and the two cars in front of him over before switching back to amber again. The driver of the Volkswagen, a more than usually law-abiding citizen, stopped so quickly that I was only just in time to prevent myself running into his back.

I sat there, frozen into helpless inactivity, to see Rupert pull up on the other side. The nearside rear door of the BMW opened, and Ralph got out holding his parcel. He walked a couple of paces forward, bent to look in at the front window and raised a hand, the grateful hitch-hiker politely thanking his benefactor. Then he turned and, without so much as a glance in my direction, disappeared out of sight down the few steps that led to the Underground station on the left.

What made matters worse was that throughout the whole

incident there had been a policeman standing by with an expression of total benevolence on his face but with his eyes fixed firmly to his front.

Then the lights changed again and we were over, for all the good that it was likely to do me now. I could get out of my car and try to catch Ralph, although I hadn't got the slightest idea as to which of the four platforms he'd be making for, or I could carry on following Rupert whose car was at least still in sight, but my whole plan depended on getting them both together. I followed Rupert, there didn't seem to be very much else to do.

Round Trafalgar Square, down Whitehall, past the Houses of Parliament, it was like following a drag line – the heart had gone out of it. Right at the roundabout into Horseferry Road, first left, on and over Vauxhall Bridge Road. Somehow I got the impression that he was trying *not* to lose me now.

It was a corner house in one of the little streets at the river end of Pimlico. There was a built-in garage forming the whole of the right-hand ground-floor half of it, and Rupert put his hand out of the window and operated a remote-control device so that the garage door swung up and over. Then he drove in, and the door lowered itself behind him, clanging shut again.

I sat looking at it for a full five minutes. Then I got out of my own car, walked up the three steps and rang the bell.

Rupert opened the door.

'You'd better come in, dear,' he said softly. He took his right hand out of his trouser pocket for long enough to let me to see his little snub-nosed automatic handgun – although his eyes looked infinitely more lethal.

'Julia's upstairs. Don't let her suspect anything unless you want me to treat her the same way.'

He ushered me past the little ground-floor dining-room on the left, up the staircase and into a sitting-room at the top.

'Look who's here, darling.'

Julia got slowly up from the armchair in which she had been sitting.

'Hello, Derek.' Her voice was hesitant.

I looked at her in silence for a moment, those grey-green eyes of hers troubled and uncertain under the sweep of silky near-blonde hair, the little tilted nose and high cheekbones, the soft perfection of her moulded lips, and I knew at once for an absolute certainty that Camberley had been right in her assessment that morning. It was Julia and only Julia that I still wanted, more than anything else in the whole world.

'Hello,' I said.

There was a Victorian watercolour of a haymaking scene in an ornate gold frame that hung on the far wall, and Rupert lifted this off its hook to reveal a little metal door behind it. Then he took a bunch of keys from his pocket with his left hand and, selecting one of them, inserted and turned it in the lock and swung the door open. Behind that again was, not the interior of a safe as I had been expecting, but a recess some four inches deep in the wall itself with a red button set in the middle of it.

'Derek's come to help me with an experiment,' he said, 'and the timing's going to be crucial. It's now four-thirty.' He pointed to the electric clock with a red sweep second-hand on the same wall, comparing it for a moment with the wrist-watch on his own hand. 'I want you, Julia, if you would be so good, to ring that bell at five o'clock precisely. Be sure to wait until the second-hand on that clock comes round exactly to the hour, because it really is absolutely vital that you don't ring it a moment before. Come on, Derek,' and he started towards the door with his right hand still in his pocket and the bunch of keys in his left hand.

Something of the tension that was existing between Rupert annd myself must have communicated itself to Julia, because she took a couple of steps towards me.

'Derek. . . . ' She paused with her lips parted slightly. Never had she looked more adorable.

I wasn't too sure of exactly what it was that Rupert had in store for me, but there was one thing of which I was certain beyond any doubt whatsoever and that was that I didn't want it to happen to her, too.

I tried to instil as much unpleasantness into the tone of my voice as I possibly could, although it nearly broke my heart to do so.

'Don't look at me,' I said. 'Talk to lover-boy here; he's in charge.'

Rupert nodded with the paternal air of one who has just detected the first faltering signs of redemption in a pair of fractious children.

'Just do as you're told, there's a good girl,' he said.

XII

WHO-WHOOP

Friday, 3 October (concluded)

The look of shocked surprise that had swept over Julia's face at the instant of my feigned rebuff to her, to be replaced in quick succession by one first of hurt and then of anger, followed me all the way as, in a state of dazed misery, I preceded Rupert out of the door of the sitting-room and down the staircase. He had taken his gun out of his pocket and now held it pointing straight at me, but I wouldn't have been able to make a move against him even if it had occurred to me at the time to do so. I know that I shall remember that look for the rest of my life.

There was a door at the bottom of the stairs on the left, and Rupert laid the muzzle of the gun against my back for a moment, as he reached past me to turn the handle, open it and switch on the lights on the far side.

There were three wooden steps beyond. At first sight, there was nothing very unusual about the garage that they led down into, except perhaps for its size. Not quite big enough for two cars, it still left a more than generous amount of space all round the silver BMW, which was parked exactly in the middle of an oil-stained concrete floor.

I walked automatically over to the front passenger-door and I was on the point of opening it when, glancing back towards Rupert, I saw him shaking his head. He locked the door through which we had come, with a clockwise movement through two full circuits, and then reached up and used the same key for the up-and-over garage-door mechanism on the ceiling, leaving the whole bunch swinging in the lock when he had done so. Finally, the gun's aim never having left my chest throughout the whole process, he pressed a black button in the middle of a little metal box that was set on the wall.

There was a slight judder of the concrete surface on which we were standing, accompanied by an unobtrusive sibilant grinding sound as of well-oiled machinery, and I stood there watching in fascination as the whole floor, carrying Rupert, myself and the BMW with it, started moving steadily downwards by means of what was now revealed to be a lift-shaft formed by a continuous projection of the garage walls.

Four chains, shiny with grease and let into the wall at either end of the two side-walls, had come into view, and it was clear that these, acting in conjunction with some sort of roller beneath the floor of the lift, formed the means of propulsion.

At first I tried to estimate just how deep we were going, but as the overhead lights of the garage above us grew progressively dimmer I soon lost track. It must have been well over a minute before I heard the sound of an engine coming up from beneath us. A similar glow, starting at our feet this time, soon became apparent, the wall to the front of the BMW gave way to a semicircular opening and, the floor of the lift drawing flush with the floor below it, we came to a scarcely noticeable stop.

We had reached our destination. I had a passing impression of a corresponding box with its black button, set on the wall in exactly the same position relative to where we were standing as the one that had been in the garage above us. But there in front of us – after all those weeks of trying to convince Camberley, now that I saw it for myself I could hardly believe it – was indeed a tunnel, some nine feet wide at ground level and lit only dimly, but stretching away in a dead-straight line in front of us until it finally disappeared into the distance far ahead.

At another gesture from Rupert, I walked out past the BMW, he following, and into the tunnel itself.

There was a metal tube running the length of its apex from which naked electric lightbulbs of about forty watts in power hung by short cobwebby lengths of flex at intervals of twenty-five yards or so. But the predominant impression now was one of complete silence, punctuated and even accentuated by a sound of soft intermittent dripping. There was a chill to the atmosphere as in that of a very deep cellar and, when I put a hand out to the concrete lining of the tunnel wall, it was damp to the touch.

We went on walking.

I was passing the second of the lightbulbs – or it could have been the third – when I noticed, just in front of me, an opening off to the right. The top and side arcs had been squared off with iron grille-work, leaving a rectangular opening which itself could be closed by means of an expanding metal gate, at present fully contracted to the left. When I reached it and was able to look through, I saw that, instead of leading to just another tunnel joining our own at right angles, as I had expected, it opened out into an intricate system of short interconnecting ones, each of a rather wider diameter than the one in which we were standing, the whole thing making up one large segmented chamber.

I stopped and gaped at it – and then back at Rupert who was close behind me.

'You don't know how privileged you are, my dear Derek.' They were the first words that he had uttered since we had left Julia behind in the first-floor sitting-room of the house at the top. 'I've never shown this to anyone before.'

'But ... who can possibly have built it all,' I said, 'and what on earth for?'

'My father did,' he replied. And, standing though we were some hundred feet below street-level in the dim light of those fantastic underground workings, so vivid was the scene as it was described to me that, even after a lapse of so many years and even at third hand, I might have been there myself as an eye-witness when Rupert Massingham went on to tell me why.

A dazzlingly clear blue sky together with the slightest of breezes made for near-perfect summer weather on that Wednesday afternoon in the first week of June 1940, as at 2.35 p.m. exactly George Massingham walked across Horse Guards Parade towards the heavy oak door near the north-west corner. He was in no hurry, because he knew that he was ten minutes early. There was an army officer already there waiting, wearing the distinctive dark khaki service-dress of the Brigade of Guards with a crown on each shoulder and a seven-flamed grenade above the near-vertical peak of his dark blue cap.

They glanced at each other warily and George wondered whether he should say something. The telephone call had certainly emphasised the importance of total confidentiality. He was still uncertain when he heard the sound of rapid footsteps coming over the tarmac behind him.

Both men turned. The figure that was approaching, raising a gold-handled stick in greeting as it did so, wearing an Anthony Eden hat, short black coat and striped trousers, soft-collared white shirt and black and white spotted bow-tie, was one that had become increasingly familiar from newsreels and newspaper photographs over the past four weeks. In real life the new Prime Minister looked rather shorter than George had imagined him to be.

'I hope I haven't kept you waiting, gentlemen,' he said. 'Mr *Mash*ingham?' He had turned to George who was in two minds as to whether or not to correct him, but he was glad that he hadn't when later he found that Mr Churchill always pronounced his S's like that. 'How good of you to come. May I introduce Major Percival?'

George and the Grenadier major shook hands, and the Prime Minister took some keys out of his fob pocket, unlocked the door and led them along a black and white mosaic-floored passage, up some stairs, across a hall and into a large drawing-room.

'This is known as the "Fish" Room,' he said. 'It has nothing to do with our piscine friends, I should tell you, even if this *is* Admiralty House. It's called after the family who presented the furniture.'

George looked up in puzzlement from the heavily ornate gilded base of one of the pieces, a sofa that he had already been studying, the principal motif of which was a formalised sea-creature of some sort.

A glint came into Mr Churchill's eye.

'Dolphins are *mammals*, Mr Massingham,' he said.

He took out a long rectangular gold cigar-case, with the letter B surmounted by an earl's coronet engraved on it, and offered it first to George who refused, then to Major Percival who took one and, finally, selected and lit one himself.

'Whisky and soda?'

The Grenadier shook his head cheerfully.

'Too early for me, I'm afraid, sir.'

It was too early for George too, but he felt awkward about saying 'no' twice running, so this time he accepted.

The Prime Minister poured it out for him, helped himself

to a very weak one at the same time and drew three of the dolphin chairs up together.

'I knew your father during the Great War,' he said when they were all settled. 'How is he?'

'Not very well,' George said. In fact Harold Massingham was to die later that same year.

'I'm sorry to hear it. The Massingham Bridge, a fine achievement. A fine achievement,' he repeated. 'Well, it's not a bridge I want from you now, Mr Massingham. Quite the reverse in fact. Tell him, Percival.'

Major Percival leant forward in his chair.

'The Prime Minister is determined that we should be ready for any eventuality. He told the House of Commons yesterday that this country would never surrender.'

George nodded. 'I read the speech in *The Times* this morning,' he said.

'In case France *should* capitulate,' went on Major Percival, 'and that in turn be followed by Germany launching a successful invasion against *us*, the Prime Minister has entrusted me with the job of recruiting a force, com-posed of civilian as well as military personnel, whose sole purpose would be to cause as much disruption to an enemy occupying power as possible. And he would like you, if you would, to be responsible for the design and construction of a secret headquarters, deep under the ground somewhere in central London, from which such a force could be led and organised. Isn't that right, sir?'

He received only a slight growl in reply from Mr Churchill, who addressed George directly.

'What do you say? Would you be prepared to take on such a task?'

Would he! It was an exciting enough prospect for any young man, and George knew that it was one that every other engineer of his acquaintance would give his ears for.

'I'd look on it as a very great honour,' he said.

'Right, then,' Major Percival continued, 'you and I can work out the details as we go along, but what I have in mind is this.'

There should be a central operations room some forty feet by forty, equipped with the best form of communications available such as a scrambler telephone network and coded radio system, with both sleeping and eating accommodation off it. Then there would have to be two completely separate entrances, both of them disguised in some way, so as to allow for quick evacuation in case one of them should be discovered, and ideally it should be accessible to an army fifteen-hundredweight truck – or, more likely, a civilian equivalent. Finally, and perhaps most important of all, so as to prevent any vital information or records falling into the hands of the enemy, it would have to possess some means of instant self-destruction as a last resort.

George's enthusiasm grew with every second that he listened. Clearly the project was going to provide a succession of challenges to his intellectual ability that would be immensely stimulating. Already, for example, ideas were forming themselves at the back of his mind as to how at least one of the entrances could be disguised so that it would be virtually undetectable.

'Why don't we site this underground headquarters somewhere close to the Thames?' he suggested. 'In that way, the two separate entrances could be either side of the river.'

Mr Churchill pulled himself up in his chair.

'Would that be possible?'

'I don't see why not,' George said.

'I felt sure that I'd chosen the right man. Be successful in this, Mr Massingham, and you, too, may find yourself in the history books some day.' The Prime Minister applied another match to the end of his cigar. 'Every facility will be made available to you,' he went on between puffs. 'Just get in touch with Major Percival here and he will arrange it. You'll each be responsible for recruiting your own personnel of course. But remember: absolute secrecy or the whole thing will be useless. This is between the three of us. Nobody else knows about this meeting. I slipped out from the garden door of Number Ten and even my private secretaries think I've come across for my usual afternoon siesta.'

He stood up and put a hand to the heavy links of the gold chain on his waistcoat, pulled a half-hunter gold watch out of its pocket, looked at it and then back at the two of them. His manner became conspiratorial.

'If I go upstairs now, I'll still have time for a bit of shut-eye. I'm a firm believer in only telling lies if it's absolutely necessary,' he said.

He led them back the way that they had come and out through the door into Horse Guards.

'Off you go, then, both of you. No time to be lost.'

'Goodbye, sir,' said the Grenadier.

'Goodbye,' George said, 'and thank you very much.'

The door had nearly shut behind them when suddenly it opened again.

'How long do you think you will need?'

It was something that George hadn't even considered yet. 'Oh, seven . . . perhaps eight months.'

Mr Churchill stood there for a moment in thought. Then, 'See if you can't make it five,' he said.

'And just how long *did* it take?' I asked Rupert.

'Six and a half months, and even that was little short of a miracle. There was a quite enormous amount to be done.'

First of all, George Massingham had had to design the main underground chamber in such a way as to fit in with Major Percival's specifications and that in itself had been no easy matter. The chamber would have to be made up of one or more subsidiary tunnels, and the only way that it proved possible to provide the necessary area of floor space without the headquarters becoming too long and unwieldy had been in the form of a Cross of Lorraine made up of three sixteen-and-a-half foot diameter tunnels – one longer with two shorter ones traversing it – the whole thing being set at right angles to the access tunnel, which itself only needed a diameter of twelve feet. The next thing had been to choose the best-possible site for it and to set about acquiring the properties that would be needed for the two separate entrances – this had not presented any very great difficulty in wartime – the house at the top from which Rupert and I had entered it and a rather larger area south of the river for the other end.

'Where the warehouse is now?' I asked.

'Oh, so you know about that, do you?' said Rupert. 'Is that what put you on to me in the first place?'

I nodded. 'That and the Glocksfoot van. Is there a lift at that end, too?'

'Not in the same way. A whole section of the front wall of the warehouse, twelve feet by twelve between two of the brick piers, descends into the ground until the top's flush with it – and that is done by a lift mechanism. But, once you're through that, you drive down to the level of the tunnel in a descending spiral.'

George Massingham had felt that having to rely on two lifts as the only means of egress would have been too claustrophobic for the people working down there so, for psychological reasons as much as those of safety, he had decided on an access road like that of a multi-storey car-park at the other end.

Finally, there had been the actual construction, and here security had been George's primary consideration. As Mr Churchill had said, if anything about the purpose of the underground system, or even of its whereabouts, were to leak out, the whole thing would become useless. Only the sinking of the main lift-shaft and the installation of the lift itself had been done from north of the river. The building of the whole length of the tunnel, together with the headquarters chamber complex, had all been carried out from the southern end.

The whole of the site south of the river had been surrounded from the outset by a twenty-foot-high wooden fence, and this had had a twenty-four-hour military guard round the outside of it. Each separate shift of workmen – and the personnel were changed several times during the course of the construction – had been collected from a central pick-up point by closed lorries, in which they were driven to a point well within the perimeter fence. The cover story given to them had been that they were building an underground air-raid shelter, designed in such a way that it could be incorporated into the London Underground Railway system after the war. The efficacy of this had been greatly enhanced by the fact that work on just such shelters was in fact started early in the following year and many of the same workmen would subsequently have been engaged on it. The drivers of the lorries, who knew *where* the site was, had been carefully segregated from their passengers, who knew *what* it was, so that no one person, being aware of both, had been in a position to make even an informed guess as to its real purpose. Deliveries of all the necessary machinery and component materials, as well as disposals of clay spoil – some eighteen hundred truck-loads of it – had been made at times when the area inside the fence had been specially cleared for the purpose. And, finally, a completely different gang of workmen had taken part in the building of the warehouse at the top.

Once it was finished, George himself had installed, first the wiring for the scrambler telephone system – the actual instruments would only be added when it was known that an invasion was imminent – and then the explosive charges that were necessary in order, as a last resort, to obliterate the underground headquarters, together with its contents and its access tunnel, by filling them with silt and water; the results of such an explosion being virtually undetectable from either the house or the warehouse at the top.

In the mean time Major Percival had been training his own subversive force elsewhere, and none of them was to be told of the facility that had been planned for them until it was needed and then only those who would actually use it. The house at the top had been bought in George Massingham's own name, and the site of the warehouse in that of a rather dull-sounding business, the ultimate owner of which would have been hard to track down and identify but would have proved to be George as well if anybody had taken the trouble to do so. There were no records in any Government department; there couldn't be – the risk of the information falling into enemy hands once an invasion had taken place would have been too great.

But by the time that the construction had been completed the danger of an invasion, and consequently of either the force or its headquarters ever being needed, had become minimal and, with the invasion of Russia in the following June and Germany being fully occupied on the Eastern Front, it had disappeared altogether. Major Percival – that hadn't even been his real name, George was to find out later – had been sent back to his regiment at his own request shortly before D-Day and had been killed soon after. Apart from himself, therefore, only Mr Churchill was now in full possession of the secret, but George wasn't to hear from him again.

The war ended, and he had waited confidently for the lists of honours to be announced. Perhaps he would even receive a peerage . . . he was already a baronet by that time,

211

remember. Something for all the selfless work and planning that he had put into it. Something at least to show for what really had been a stupendous engineering achievement. But there had been nothing. George Massingham came out of the war as he had gone into it, the relatively unknown and totally undistinguished son of a famous father. He had still been on the payroll, that was one consolation – the cheques, such as they were, had kept on coming in.

Perhaps Mr Churchill had forgotten all about it, George had been fair enough to concede that he had plenty of other things to think about. Or perhaps he did remember – he was already foreseeing trouble with Russia, and he might have taken a conscious decision to avoid doing the slightest thing that might have jeopardised its secrecy, in case the need for it and the subversive force that was to use it should arise for a second time. However it was, the disappointment proved too much for George Massingham. What was the use of bothering? He only ever bothered over one more thing again.

'He was determined to send me to Eton, as he had been sent by his own father. Scrimped and saved in order to do so, and I think the fact that he managed it did at least give him a certain amount of satisfaction. Then, shortly before he died, he brought me down here and showed it all to me – just as I'm showing it to you – the last great undiscovered secret of the '39–'45 war.'

George had been promised a place in the history books, like his father before him. And now, as his own son described them to me, I could almost feel myself the successive emotions as he must have gone through them. The initial pride of achievement, the sure hope of recognition and all that that would lead to, the gradual disillusionment that led to eventual apathy and hopelessness, the feeling of total rejection – that must have been the cruellest of all.

'Poor old boy,' I said.

Rupert snorted.

'Poor old boy nothing. Silly old fool, more like. If you want something in this world badly enough, you've got to go out and get it for yourself. What's the good of leaving it to others and then spending the rest of your life whining about it?' he said.

The bitterness in his tone brought me instantly back to the present. There we both were in the dim light of the tunnel, standing by the gated opening to the underground head-quarters. Rupert's gun had still never wavered from its aim.

'That's all very well,' I said, 'but don't you think that planning a coup to bring down the Government might be carrying that philosophy just a little too far?'

He stared at me in genuine astonishment.

'Coup? Bring down the Government? What on earth are you talking about, Derek?'

'Do you seriously mean to tell me that you weren't trying to kill the Prime Minister this afternoon?'

'Don't be silly, dear.' Rupert's face had resumed its normal expression of slightly pitying superiority. 'If you hadn't interfered when you did, nobody would have been in the slightest danger – let alone hurt in any way.'

'What *did* you mean to happen, then?'

'It's quite simple. Charles Fortescue was to have been hustled off downstairs in the same way that we were. An ashtray would have been found at the place where the fire started and people would have remembered seeing him stubbing one of his cigarettes out in that exact place. It's common gossip he's already started a couple of fires acci-dentally. Someone who can't even the control the effects of his own over-indulgence in a habit that is of itself rep-rehensible, putting a little girl's life at risk and then saving

213

himself without a thought for her. Is that really the sort of man you want to have running the country for you? How do you think that would have looked in the newspapers? He wouldn't have lasted as Prime Minister more than a couple of days.'

'Whereas now he's a national hero,' I said.

'Yes, damn you.'

He paused.

Then: 'Charles would have retired in a year or two, in any case. Sooner, possibly. I was just hurrying things along a bit – and that's all I've been doing all along.'

'Apart from indulging in a spot of blackmail on the side,' I said.

Rupert gave a short laugh.

'Yes, Dorothy Elton brought you in on that one, didn't she? Contrary to my strict instructions, I may say, that's why I screwed the extra ten thousand out of her. I did give that back, you know.'

'But you still kept the first fifty.'

'No, that went straight off, canvas bag and all, to Oxfam. Poetic justice, I thought. It was sheer fraud what she was up to with that first husband of hers, the other George, and I couldn't let her get away without paying something for her part in that.'

My immediate thought was how ironic it was that Rupert's views should have coincided so nearly with Dorothy's own over this particular aspect of the matter. But then it struck me that here at last was the answer to one of the principal riddles concerning Rupert's conduct.

'So that was all part of the same thing, too?'

'Yes, John Elton was looking like being unstoppable when I was dining with old Wally Bagley one evening and he got out those papers of his and told me the story. Old fool didn't realise their significance, but I did. I happened to know that Dorothy's jewellery was entailed. Sheer luck,

214

because John himself hardly ever puts a foot wrong and I'd never have got anything on him like the others.

'But wouldn't it have been easier just to send the papers off to the press in the first place?'

'I couldn't do that.' Rupert sounded genuinely shocked.

'Why not?'

'Why not? My dear Derek, the Eltons are friends of mine,' he said.

I was beginning to suspect that I was now supplying the one element that had been lacking to Rupert in his progress so far: an audience to be impressed by his cleverness. But this could just react to my own advantage. The longer I could keep him talking, the more chance I might have.

'You mentioned others. Who were they?'

'Peter White for a start, he was the next biggest hurdle after John. You saw me do my best to stop him making a fool of himself over USCRODD at Home Affairs that day, well, I thought I might as well make use of it, so I arranged for four young friends of mine to go up to that demonstration at Mathersdon and start something – you know them, I think.'

'Ralph and his friends? I'd been wondering about them. How did you manage to get hold of them in the first place?'

'They tried to mug me in the street one day much the same as they did you, later. I gave them a choice, the contents of my wallet or a weekly retainer. You'd be surprised how loyal and discreet they've been since then.'

I nodded.

In fact I had severe doubts about this last statement. I was pretty sure by now that it had been them, boasting among their criminal confrères, that had led to the tipping-off of Camberley Roberts. But, if I were to allow myself the satisfaction of disillusioning Rupert, I would certainly be running the risk of alerting him as to Camberley's real part in all this.

'Then there was that chap, what's-his-name, caught out in the unsavoury Soho nightclub,' he went on. 'That was the first job they did for me.'

'And it was you who persuaded Patrick Oldfield to come up to the Lords, so he was safely out of it?'

'Yes, best place for him. But some of my colleagues have been falling over themselves to be helpful. Those three since July had nothing to do with me.'

'And Bobby Digby getting embroiled with Honoria. I suppose he came into that category?'

'No, oddly enough Bobby was the easiest of the lot. I gave a small dinner-party for the Digbys and didn't even invite Honoria. I just asked along her current admirer, told him to bring a friend, sat her and Bobby next to one another at dinner and left the rest to them.'

'With a little bit of help from the newspapers?'

Rupert gave a slight shrug to his shoulders.

'You'll always find some rag that's prepared to be the first to publish and, once a story's broken, even the papers that like to think of themselves as respectable can't wait to dabble their inky little fingers in someone's political lifeblood.'

Whatever my own views on the subject, I didn't think it was up to Rupert Massingham of all people to take such a high moral attitude over something like that.

'That's all very well,' I said, 'but with some of them it's been actual lifeblood. Bobby Digby for one.'

'Yes, I was sorry about Bobby, but it was hardly my fault. All I've done is to facilitate weaknesses that were already there and would have come out sooner or later in any case. With Bobby it could have happened at any time. That little bitch of a wife of his, Jenny, would have seen to that.'

'What about that girl at lunch-time? It was only by the grace of God that she wasn't suffocated.'

'Penny-Sweet?' Rupert's eyes glinted. 'So that would have been a loss? No, I'd taken the trouble to pay an official visit to the Halverton Fire Brigade earlier this morning, warned them to be on their toes with the eyes of the world on them while the PM was there. Only, in the original scenario it was I who was to have rescued her and been the hero of the hour.'

'The Terrier-men, then. Ted very nearly died, and you were certainly the direct cause of Tom's death.'

'*I* was? My dear Derek, my chaps didn't start it; *they* did. And, if anyone was responsible for what happened to them, *you* were. It was you who brought them in in the first place.'

I had one last try. Somehow Rupert was managing to twist everything that I said until he almost had me believing him myself.

'Well, there *were* four people killed during those anti-nuclear demonstrations up at Mathersdon. You admit that you set in train the disturbances there and that makes you guilty of murder – manslaughter, at any rate. Even you can't talk your way out of that.'

He shook his head impatiently. 'Don't give me all that crap about guilt. Nobody asked those people to go up there and demonstrate and politicians have to make decisions every day of their lives that are going to mean the difference between life and death for somebody. Add to that the fact that no one deserves to get to the top in politics unless he's prepared to take the sort of risks that I have. Look, Derek, I've got something to give and I owe it to the country to see that I'm in a position to give it.'

I don't think that it was until that moment that I knew just how mad Rupert Massingham really was. It wasn't so much that he had done all the things he had for his own advancement, as that he was now glorying in, and making a virtue out of, the fact that he had been prepared to do them. And this was the man who, within a matter of months, was going to be the country's next Prime Minister. Only this morning it would have been days or even hours.

'But . . . you're the natural successor to Charles Fortescue. Why couldn't you have waited?' I said. 'You'd have got there in the end.'

'Would I? Would you have said that seven or eight months ago?'

I thought back to my luncheon at White's with Jimmy McKay.

'Possibly not. I would now, though.'

'But don't you see – now's the very last time to stop. There's a General Election coming up, and this country simply can't afford five years of a left-wing Labour government. Let alone the well-intentioned woolliness of an Alliance one.'

'Has it occurred to you that we might win the election even without you as Prime Minister?'

Again, that short dry laugh of his.

'What, with Charles Fortescue to lead us? Never! Charlie-boy couldn't lead a dog into a butcher's shop.'

'Meaning you could?'

'You know I can,' he said. 'But if there's one thing I did learn from my father's life it's that mere possession of merit and ability isn't enough. Opportunities don't just come to you in this world, you've got to go out and make them for yourself. Which brings me back to you.'

'Me?'

'Yes. I'm sorry, Derek, I really am, but I simply daren't take the risk of everything I've worked for being jeopardised by you constantly harassing me. It's a pity, because you could have had Julia back, too. She was becoming a bit of a bore.'

218

With what I knew of Rupert now, I couldn't be sure whether that last bit was even meant as an insult, but I was determined not to rise to it just in case.

'Would it do any good', I said, 'if I promised to keep my mouth shut?'

He shook his head.

'No, principally because when it came to it you'd never bring yourself to give such an undertaking, knowing you wouldn't be able to keep it. That's the difference between us. *I* would . . . and be sure I was doing my duty as I broke it.'

He gestured with his gun hand towards the opening in the iron grille-work.

'Now, just step backwards, very slowly and carefully, to the other side of that gate, will you?'

Something about the movement brought the drill with the knife, from my initial tuition in the police gymnasium, flashing back into my mind.

Hands raised, pivot on left heel, right foot back and sideways, thereby reducing target area.

Without having made a conscious decision to do so, I had gone into the routine that Camberley had taught me to make automatic.

Drop right hand on to assailant's, avoiding weapon, and grip to immobilise fingers.

The separate moves followed one after another in an instant, but I myself was seeing the whole thing as in slow motion.

Spin hand round so that palm uppermost, my left arm under assailant's right, grab own wrist, force right hand down, left arm up, causing assailant first drop weapon. . . .

The gun fell with a clatter to the concrete floor.

. . . then, as body arches forward, right knee into solar plexus.

It was here that there was an unexpected bonus. Rupert, in falling, hit his head on the grille-work at the side and,

219

dropping to the ground, stayed there dazed and motionless for a moment. I bundled him through the gap, slammed the expanding gate shut behind him, picked up the gun from where it had fallen and stood waiting.

The expression on the face of this extraordinary man as he got to his feet, rubbing the dirt off the knees of his trousers as he did so, was one of pure ungrudging admiration.

'Well *done*, Derek. I didn't know you had it in you,' he said.

He reached a hand forward to the expanding gate and shook it. I raised my hand slightly so that he couldn't miss seeing the gun in it.

'Steady,' I said.

I needn't have worried. The gate remained firmly shut.

'Er . . . Derek, we seem to have a bit of a problem. This gate's self-locking, and I haven't got the key on me.'

I took a tighter grip on the gun.

'I'll go up and get it. Is it on the ring with the others?'

'No, don't do that. The whole tunnel's due to blow at any moment. Nip up, there's a good chap, and stop Julia pressing that button. You wouldn't want her to have my death on her conscience,' he said.

'What! You don't mean . . . ?' It took a moment or two for the full enormity of what he was saying to get through to me.

'Yes, neat, wasn't it? But it seems to have misfired somewhat.' He looked at his watch. 'Don't hang about, dear; you've only got three minutes.'

He made it sound as though it were I who would be the sufferer rather than he.

I turned and ran back down the tunnel. I was almost at the lift when I heard him call out after me.

'If she won't listen to you, tell her you have my authority,' he said.

Even as this last rankled, just as this time I knew that it was meant to, I couldn't but admire him for it. It might well have goaded me into letting things take their course – heaven knows it would have been justified – or at least have delayed me for just long enough to be those few vital seconds too late. He had been right about one thing, though, the last thing I wanted was for Julia to have to live with something like that.

The lift seemed to take an age in its journey upwards and, once at the top, I had to force myself to act calmly and methodically as I unlocked the door into the main part of the house, turning the key full cycle twice. Then I rushed through it and thundered up the stairs, slamming the door of the sitting-room open with a resounding crash. Julia had her back to me, but I could have sworn that her hand was actually moving towards the button.

'For God's sake stop,' I said.

She turned, and there was no sign of welcome on her face as she did so. But her eyes softened as I told her the whole story, how I had come into it – realising that I was breaking my promise to Dorothy as I did so, but I had no choice now and I swore her to secrecy – what Camberley and I had discovered, what we had worked out for ourselves, the revelations in the tunnel and, finally, about the tunnel itself with its built-in abort system.

'Then, that button . . . ?'

I nodded.

'Oh my God,' she said.

She came into my arms, stiff and shaking, put her head on my shoulder and broke into great heaving sobs. I held her tight against me with one hand and stroked her hair with the other. The tears gradually lessened until at last they stopped altogether as I felt her whole body relax.

Then, gently, she disengaged herself and looked up at me.

221

'But . . . why? Why did Rupert want *me* to press the button when he could have been up here in time to do it himself anyway?'

I'd been wondering about that myself.

'Three reasons, I think. Partly fastidiousness: he always seemed to prefer to get someone else – that gang of his, for instance – to do his dirty work for him. And partly as a sort of insurance, if anyone found out about it he could always have said that you'd misunderstood him. But I can't help feeling he might have been getting an added kick out of the fact that it was you he was making do it.'

'Oh, Derek . . . '

I stopped her, putting a finger to her lips.

Then I took the gold ring with its Mallicent Owl and sprig of three roses off my little finger and held it up, questioningly, for her to see.

'May I have my ring back . . . Derek . . . please?'

She held her right hand out towards me, fingers slightly apart, and then, shyly, hesitantly, offered as an alternative, her left.

I put my father's signet ring on the third finger of Julia's left hand.

She came into my arms again, and this time all the soft curves of her body moulded themselves against me as she put up her mouth to be kissed.

Minutes passed.

And then, even at that time of supreme happiness, I found myself unable to prevent the seemingly insoluble problem of Rupert from creeping back into my mind. I knew exactly how it would be. I'd go down there and find him glancing ostentatiously at his wrist-watch.

'You took your time, dear,' he would say. I could almost hear the tone that would be in his voice and see the expression on his face as he said it.

What then?

We now knew exactly what he'd been up to all these months, but we still hadn't got a shred of evidence to prove it. We knew of the existence of the tunnel of course, but, although that had been the indirect means of my first getting wind of Rupert's activities, as far as we knew he never actually used it in connection with any of them. And I'd only be getting myself into trouble if I revealed what was undoubtedly a legitimate State Secret.

I could always go and have another try with Tom Lavenham, my Chief Whip, or even Patrick Oldfield, but I remembered all too vividly the reception I had got last time. True, I'd have Camberley Roberts to back me up, but could I really see myself doing any better now?

As far as the blackmail was concerned, even if I really broke my promise to Dorothy Elton and bullied her into talking, she never actually saw Rupert collect the money, and the same applied to Cully and poor old Ted.

Then there was the business down at Halverton, but Rupert Massingham would by now have had all the time he needed to make up a story convincing enough to account for his actions. Mad he might be, but he was clever enough to know that we still hadn't got anything like enough to stop him.

If only Camberley and that police inspector friend of hers had actually managed to catch up with Rupert earlier this same day, with the shock of surprise they might just have been able to force some sort of confession out of him.

If only I myself had succeeded in catching the odious Ralph with that incriminating parcel of his still on him.

If only . . .

No, sooner rather than later, Charles Fortescue would give up as Prime Minister, and who but Rupert could succeed him?

And then?

Rupert Massingham had been on his best behaviour politically so far – he'd had to be – but I was pretty certain by this time that watching that brilliant father of his decline into first disillusion, then apathy and finally hopelessness had made him so obsessed with the necessity for himself to succeed that he had become little short of a psychopath. The main difficulty, Sam Appleby had told me that afternoon in the House of Lords library, would lie in getting to power in the first place. Was it conceivable now that Rupert would stop at anything in order to keep himself there, a man who had lied and cheated and even killed his way to the top?

The entire police force, whose attitude would be crucial, seemed to have fallen for him, and now they had USCRODD, the Ultra-Sonic Crowd Dispersal Device, which Rupert himself had already used to such effect as Home Secretary. The future rolled out before me with an awful sense of inevitability. I had a nasty feeling that that might just be the one additional factor that Sam had predicted a potential dictator might need.

I took the bunch of keys out of my pocket, tossed them an inch or two up into the air and caught them again.

'I'd better go and let the bastard out,' I said. 'It's got to be done some time, I suppose. Though I almost wish now that I *hadn't* got back up here in time to stop you pressing the button.'

Julia stared at me.

'But . . . don't you understand, Derek? You didn't. I'd already pressed it,' she said.

In Greater London there are twelve tunnels under the River Thames.